Leo and the Leaf Pile

Adventure

Nora Black

Published by Lightwave Publishing, 2024.

This is a work of fiction. Similarities to real people, places, or events are entirely coincidental.

LEO AND THE LEAF PILE

First edition. November 18, 2024.

Copyright © 2024 Nora Black.

ISBN: 979-8230079781

Written by Nora Black.

Table of Contents

Preface 1
Chapter 1: The Big Leaf Pile Idea 2
Chapter 2: Gathering Leaves 6
Chapter 3: Friends Notice the Pile 10
Chapter 4: The First Jump 14
Chapter 5: A Little Visitor 17
Chapter 6: The Leaf Dance 21
Chapter 7: Bramble's Invitation 25
Chapter 8: An Unexpected Mess 29
Chapter 9: The Leaf Game Rules 33
Chapter 10: A Surprise for Nettle 37
Chapter 11: The Best Jump Contest 41
Chapter 12: A Little Visitor 45
Chapter 13: A Lost Leaf 49
Chapter 14: The Leaf Lantern Idea 53
Chapter 15: The Stormy Surprise 58
Chapter 16: The Hidden Hollow 62
Chapter 17: A Visitor from Afar 67
Chapter 18: The Festival of Friendship 72
Chapter 19: The Story of the Valley 76
Chapter 20: The Mysterious Marks 81
Chapter 21: The Memory Book 85
Chapter 22: Preparing for the Harvest Gathering 90
Chapter 23: A Visitor from Beyond the Valley 96
Chapter 24: A Special Welcome for Quill 100
Chapter 25: A Journey of Friendship 105

Preface

Friendship, kindness, and wonder are gifts that transform everyday moments into cherished memories.

Leo and the Leaf Pile was inspired by the idea that life's greatest joys are often simple—sharing laughter, offering a helping hand, or just enjoying a quiet moment together. This book invites readers to join Leo and his friends as they learn the beauty of community in the Valley of Echoes. Their adventures, challenges, and heartwarming discoveries echo timeless values of love, gratitude, and acceptance, which we hope will resonate with readers of all ages.

May this story spark smiles and serve as a gentle reminder that friendship is a treasure, worth celebrating every day.

Chapter 1: The Big Leaf Pile Idea

In a quiet corner of the Valley of Echoes, where the sun dappled the ground in a kaleidoscope of colors, a young squirrel named Ember had an idea. Autumn had swept through the valley, painting the trees in every shade of red, gold, and amber. The leaves had fallen in thick, crunchy layers, covering the forest floor like a grand, colorful blanket. As Ember scurried through the leaves, gathering his favorite acorns and hopping over fallen branches, he looked around and thought about what he could do with all the leaves lying about.

Ember loved the feeling of leaves crunching beneath his paws. He'd often tumble and roll, delighted by the soft, crinkly sound. But today, Ember wanted something bigger, something grander—a leaf pile unlike any other. The kind of leaf pile that would tower above his head and let him leap into it with all his might. Yes, that would be perfect!

He scurried back to his little tree hollow to grab a few supplies. With his tiny woven basket and a determined glint in his eyes, Ember set off to gather as many leaves as he could find. He would search every corner of the valley, every nook and cranny, to find the best, fluffiest, and brightest leaves for his pile.

As he hopped from one tree to the next, Ember gathered handfuls of leaves—big, small, golden, and red. He collected soft leaves from the oaks, crinkly ones from the maples, and even a few sweet-smelling leaves from a patch of mint plants that grew along the riverbank. His basket was quickly filling up, but Ember was only just getting started. He wanted his pile to be big enough for the biggest jump he'd ever taken. He imagined himself soaring through the air, arms spread wide, and landing with a satisfying "whump!" right in the center of his grand leaf pile.

Hours passed, and soon Ember had built up a small mound of leaves at the base of an ancient oak tree. But a small mound wasn't nearly enough. Ember wanted a pile so big that he could barely see over it! He wanted a pile so huge that it would be the talk of the entire valley.

As Ember worked, he didn't notice a pair of small eyes watching him from behind a bush. Blossom, a shy little mouse with soft brown fur and bright eyes, had been watching Ember build his pile for some time. She admired his determination and couldn't help but feel a bit excited herself as the pile grew bigger and bigger. But Blossom was shy, and she wasn't sure if she should approach Ember and ask to join in the fun.

Ember, however, was lost in his own world of leaf-piling, and the idea of sharing his leaf pile hadn't yet crossed his mind. He carefully placed each leaf in his growing pile, rearranging and fluffing the leaves to make sure they were just right. Ember stood back and admired his work. His leaf pile was, at last, starting to look like something truly grand.

Meanwhile, other animals in the forest had begun to notice Ember's creation. One by one, they peeked out from their homes and bushes, curious about the growing leaf pile. There was Fern, the young hedgehog with a curious streak, and Lark, the cheerful chipmunk who loved any excuse for a game. Even Meadow, the wise old turtle, had wandered over to take a look, her slow, steady steps bringing her closer to the impressive pile of leaves.

Ember noticed them too, though he hadn't considered inviting them to join just yet. His mind was filled with images of his spectacular jump, of the leaves scattering all around him as he landed right in the center of his creation. But then he saw Blossom, hesitating by the edge of the pile, her eyes wide with a mix of wonder and longing.

"Hi, Blossom!" Ember called out, waving a paw. "What do you think of my leaf pile? Isn't it the biggest you've ever seen?"

Blossom smiled shyly, her tiny paws fiddling with the edge of her scarf. "It's amazing, Ember. I've never seen anything like it." She paused, looking down at the ground before glancing back up at him. "It... it looks like it would be so much fun to jump in."

Ember hadn't thought about anyone else jumping in his pile. He imagined all the leaves scattering, the pile getting messy, and his perfect leaf-jumping experience changing. But as he looked at Blossom's hopeful face, a strange thought crept into his mind. Perhaps, just perhaps, it might be more fun to share the pile with a friend.

"You know, Blossom," he said slowly, "it might be fun to jump in together."

Blossom's face lit up with a smile, and she nodded eagerly. She took a few hesitant steps toward the leaf pile, her eyes sparkling with excitement. Ember felt a warm, happy feeling as he watched her approach. Maybe this would be even better than he had planned.

With a little whoop of excitement, Ember counted to three, and together, they took a running leap into the leaf pile. Leaves flew in every direction, and the two friends tumbled, giggling, through the soft, rustling pile. They kicked, they rolled, and they tossed leaves into the air with wild abandon. Ember's careful pile was quickly transformed into a chaotic, joyful mess, and he couldn't remember a time when he'd felt happier.

As they lay in the leaves, catching their breath and laughing, Ember looked over at Blossom. "You know," he said, "I think this pile is even better when it's shared. I was so excited to jump in by myself, but jumping with you made it twice as fun."

Blossom beamed, her cheeks rosy with joy. "I think so too, Ember. It's the most fun I've had in a long time."

The two friends spent the rest of the afternoon playing in the leaves, creating games, and laughing until their sides hurt. They forgot about making a perfect pile or having the biggest jump; instead, they discovered the simple joy of sharing the moment with someone else. They lay side by side in the scattered leaves, grateful for the fun they had shared.

That night, as Ember curled up in his cozy tree hollow, he thought back to his day. His pile hadn't turned out quite as he had imagined—it was scattered, messy, and much smaller than it had been at the start. But it had become something far better than a grand leaf pile. It had become a place for friends to laugh and play together, and that made it even more special.

Ember drifted off to sleep with a contented smile, dreaming of more days filled with leaves, laughter, and friends.

Chapter 2: Gathering Leaves

Early the next morning, Ember was up before the sun peeked over the trees. As the first rays of sunlight spilled across the valley, he could hardly contain his excitement to continue building his leaf pile. After yesterday's adventure with Blossom, Ember felt inspired to make his leaf pile even bigger and better than before. He wasn't sure exactly how he'd top the pile they'd already enjoyed, but he was eager to try.

With a deep breath, Ember stretched his tiny arms and scampered down from his tree hollow. His tail flicked with determination, and his little basket hung from one paw, ready for another day of collecting the best leaves the valley had to offer.

He dashed to the nearby oak tree, where a fresh batch of leaves had fallen overnight. Each one was perfectly crinkly and richly colored, glowing under the early morning light. Ember grinned as he plucked them up, one by one, placing them in his basket. He wanted this pile to be massive, more impressive than even the one he and Blossom had shared.

As he worked, he thought about yesterday. The joy he had felt while playing in the leaves with Blossom was still fresh in his memory. Part of him was excited to share his new pile with more friends, but he still wasn't entirely sure. After all, there was something magical about having his very own leaf pile, just for himself. Yet, even as he thought about keeping it private, he felt a tug of warmth at the thought of his friends laughing and playing alongside him.

With a shake of his head, Ember pushed the thought aside. First, he needed to finish the pile. Decisions could come later.

By the time he finished at the oak tree, his basket was overflowing with leaves. There were golden leaves, bright red ones, and even a few that sparkled in the sunlight as though touched by a dusting of dew. As he made his way back to the clearing, Ember's nose caught a familiar scent—berries. A small berry bush sat near his path, and Ember stopped, his mouth watering. Gathering leaves was hard work, after all, and a snack would be perfect.

But as he reached out to pluck a berry, he heard a gentle rustle from the other side of the bush. Curiously, he peered over and saw Luna, a young fox with a soft coat and a clever glint in her eyes. She was sniffing the bush, clearly hoping for a snack too.

"Oh, hello, Luna!" Ember greeted her, feeling his whiskers twitch with surprise. "I didn't see you there!"

Luna looked up, her nose twitching as she noticed Ember's basket of leaves. She tilted her head, her eyes narrowing playfully. "Ember! Are you collecting leaves again? Didn't you have a big pile yesterday?"

Ember nodded proudly, patting his basket. "I did, but I'm making an even bigger one today. It's going to be the best leaf pile in the whole valley!" He held his head high, feeling a surge of pride.

Luna's eyes sparkled with interest. "That sounds like fun! Are you building it for everyone to play in?"

Ember hesitated, shifting his weight from one paw to the other. He hadn't really thought about whether this pile would be for everyone or just for him. The thought of having his own leaf pile, one that was untouched and perfectly crafted, was still quite appealing. But then he remembered the laughter and joy of sharing it with Blossom yesterday.

"I... I haven't decided yet," he said slowly. "I was kind of planning on making it for myself, but maybe I'll share it. I'm not sure yet."

Luna's face softened, and she nodded understandingly. "I know the feeling. Sometimes it's nice to have something that's just yours. But sharing can be special too." With a wink, she leaned closer, picking a berry from the bush and nibbling it. "Well, if you need any help gathering leaves, let me know. I'd love to see this grand pile of yours when it's ready!"

Ember thanked her, and with his basket full, he continued on his way. As he walked, he thought about Luna's words. Sharing could indeed be special, but it was hard to balance that with his desire for something uniquely his. He sighed, deciding to push the thought aside until later.

As the sun climbed higher in the sky, Ember's leaf pile grew larger. Every time he thought he'd gathered enough, he found another patch of leaves, too beautiful to leave behind. Soon, his pile was enormous, even bigger than the one from the day before. It was taller than he was, nearly reaching his favorite branch in the nearby oak.

Just as he was about to test his new pile with a jump, he heard a cheerful chattering sound. Looking up, he saw Bramble, a young hedgehog, rolling towards him. Bramble loved rolling everywhere he went, using his quills to gather leaves and sticks as he tumbled. Ember grinned as Bramble rolled to a stop right in front of him, shaking the leaves from his back.

"Hey, Ember!" Bramble squeaked, his little eyes bright with excitement. "Are you making a leaf pile? That looks amazing!"

Ember puffed out his chest proudly. "I am! I've been collecting leaves all morning. I want it to be the biggest and best leaf pile in the valley."

Bramble clapped his tiny paws together, hopping up and down. "Can I help? I love gathering leaves! And maybe... maybe we could play in it together when it's done?"

Ember's heart softened at Bramble's eagerness. Part of him still wanted to have the pile to himself, but he couldn't deny the joy he felt when he thought about playing with his friends again. He took a deep breath, considering his options. Maybe sharing wasn't about giving up what he wanted; maybe it was about making something even more enjoyable with others.

"Alright, Bramble," he said with a smile, "let's make this pile together. It'll be the biggest pile we've ever seen, and we'll jump in together!"

Bramble squealed with delight, and the two friends set to work, gathering more leaves and carefully adding them to the pile. They

LEO AND THE LEAF PILE 9

found leaves of every color and shape, even some with speckled patterns that looked like tiny works of art. As they worked, Ember found himself relaxing, laughing with Bramble over silly things and enjoying the camaraderie. Building the pile was more fun with a friend by his side.

Ember and Bramble had created a truly impressive pile. It was nearly as tall as they were, wide and fluffy, perfect for jumping into. Ember stood back to admire it, his heart swelling with pride and gratitude.

Chapter 3: Friends Notice the Pile

The sun had barely risen over the Valley of Echoes when Ember finished placing the last leaf on his massive pile. The leaf pile, which he had been building for days now, towered high above his head. It was bigger, fluffier, and brighter than any other pile he'd ever seen, with colors so vibrant it looked as though a rainbow had settled on the forest floor.

As Ember admired his work, he felt a swell of pride. He remembered the fun he had shared with Blossom and Bramble, the two friends who had helped him gather leaves and play in the pile. It had felt special to share his creation, and he was excited to show it off even more. But Ember wasn't sure if he was ready for the attention of everyone else in the valley.

Just as he was thinking about it, he heard the sound of soft hopping. Zinnia, the lively rabbit with fur as soft as dandelion fluff, came bounding over a hill, her large ears perked up in curiosity. She froze, eyes widening, when she saw the magnificent pile of leaves.

"Oh, Ember!" Zinnia cried, hopping closer with bright, excited eyes. "Is this your leaf pile? It's so big, I thought it was a hill from a distance! I could see it from my burrow near the stream!"

Ember grinned proudly. "It is, Zinnia! I've been working on it for days. It's the biggest one I've ever made."

Zinnia bounded over to the pile, her nose twitching as she sniffed the sweet scent of autumn leaves. "It's amazing! And it looks so soft and fluffy. Could... could I jump in it too?"

Ember hesitated, remembering how much fun it had been to share the pile with Blossom and Bramble. The idea of Zinnia joining in felt like it would make the experience even better. Still, he had worked hard on this pile and wanted it to stay perfect.

"Yes, you can," he finally said with a smile. "But maybe let's wait a little longer. I think more friends might want to join us!"

Zinnia's eyes sparkled with excitement, and she clapped her paws together in delight. "Thank you, Ember! I can't wait! I'll go tell everyone else!"

With a joyful bounce, Zinnia dashed off, her fluffy tail trailing behind her as she hurried to spread the word. Ember chuckled as he watched her disappear over the hill. Part of him was nervous about sharing his pile with so many others, but he also couldn't deny the thrill of knowing they'd all be enjoying it together.

Before long, other animals started arriving, one by one, each drawn by the rumors of Ember's enormous leaf pile. First came Hazel, the young fox cub with a sleek, reddish-brown coat and curious eyes. She sniffed around the pile, her tail swishing with excitement.

"Wow, Ember!" Hazel said, her voice filled with awe. "I've never seen anything like this! It looks like it would be so much fun to jump in."

Ember puffed out his chest, feeling a mix of pride and excitement. "I worked hard to make it big enough for everyone to enjoy," he said. "This way, we can all jump in together!"

Hazel's eyes lit up, and she wagged her tail. "Really? Oh, thank you, Ember! I can't wait to jump in!"

As Hazel examined the pile, Ember noticed a small figure peeking from behind a tree. It was Thorn, the shy hedgehog who always carried a tiny leaf umbrella, even on sunny days. Thorn often stayed hidden, too nervous to join in on big gatherings, but today he seemed drawn to the pile like a moth to a flame.

"Hey, Thorn!" Ember called, waving a paw. "Do you want to come over and see the leaf pile?"

Thorn shuffled closer, his little feet rustling the leaves. He glanced at the pile, his eyes wide with wonder, before looking up at Ember. "It's... it's very big," he said softly, his voice barely above a whisper. "I'd like to jump in, but... I'm not very good at jumping."

Ember smiled gently and patted Thorn's shoulder. "That's okay, Thorn. You can roll in, or even just sit on the edge. The pile is for everyone to enjoy, however they want!"

Thorn's face broke into a shy smile, and he nodded, feeling a bit braver with Ember's encouragement.

As the morning wore on, more animals arrived, all drawn by Zinnia's excited chatter and the sight of the impressive leaf pile. Midge, the magpie, fluttered down from the treetops, her glossy feathers gleaming in the sunlight. She circled the pile, eyeing the colorful leaves with interest.

"Oh, Ember, it's beautiful!" she chirped. "And I heard you're letting everyone join in. That's so generous of you!"

Ember grinned, feeling a warm glow in his chest. "Thank you, Midge! I just thought it would be even more fun if we all jumped together."

Midge nodded approvingly, her beady eyes gleaming with excitement. "You're absolutely right! I'll go spread the word to the other birds. I'm sure they'd love to join us!"

And off she flew, her wings flapping as she headed into the trees to tell the rest of the valley's bird population. Ember watched her go, feeling a mix of excitement and nervousness. So many animals were interested in his leaf pile. Would it be able to handle everyone?

As he pondered this, a shadow passed overhead, and Ember looked up to see Willow, the wise old owl, gliding gracefully toward the pile. Willow had lived in the valley for longer than most of the animals, and her feathers shimmered in shades of brown and gray as she settled on a branch nearby, looking down at Ember and the leaf pile with an approving gaze.

"You've built something wonderful here, young Ember," Willow hooted, her voice calm and steady. "It reminds me of the grand leaf piles we used to make when I was a young owl."

Ember's eyes sparkled with curiosity. "You used to make leaf piles too, Willow?"

"Oh, yes," Willow replied, her eyes crinkling with amusement. "We would gather all the leaves we could find and invite everyone in the valley to jump and play. The pile didn't last very long, but the memories we made were worth more than any pile."

Ember thought about her words, realizing that Willow's memories were just as important as the pile itself. His heart swelled as he looked at the animals gathering around his pile, their faces alight with excitement.

Just then, Hazel, Thorn, and Zinnia all lined up, ready to take the first leap. Ember stood in the center, his eyes wide with joy as he watched his friends, each waiting for his signal.

"Alright, everyone!" Ember called, his voice loud and clear. "On the count of three, let's jump together!"

The animals prepared, their excitement bubbling over. Some wiggled their paws, others flapped their wings, and even Thorn, the shy little hedgehog, looked ready to give it his best effort.

"One... two... THREE!" Ember shouted, and with a collective leap, they all jumped into the pile.

The valley filled with sounds of laughter and joy as the animals tumbled and rolled through the leaves. Some leaped, others twirled, and a few simply sat back, enjoying the view as leaves scattered everywhere. The pile was no longer perfect and neat; it was a colorful whirlwind of fun, laughter, and friendship.

Chapter 4: The First Jump

The setting sun cast a warm, golden light across the valley as the animals gathered around Ember's enormous leaf pile. After days of collecting leaves, encouraging friends to join in, and witnessing the excitement of his fellow animals, Ember felt a sense of pride and anticipation. They were about to have their first real jump, and he couldn't wait to experience it alongside his friends.

Ember stood in the center of the crowd, looking around at the eager faces of his friends. Zinnia the rabbit, Hazel the fox, Midge the magpie, and Thorn the hedgehog had each played a part in building the pile, and now they all stood ready to leap together. He noticed others too, like Luna the fox and Fern the chipmunk, who had heard about the pile from Zinnia and come to join in on the fun.

Ember raised a paw to gather everyone's attention. "Alright, everyone!" he called out, his voice brimming with excitement. "This is it—the first big jump! Let's make it a good one!"

A cheer went up from the crowd, and Ember felt a wave of happiness sweep over him. He had built this pile with love and care, but it was the enthusiasm of his friends that made it truly special. He lined up with them, ready to count down to their first jump.

"On the count of three!" he shouted. "One... two... THREE!"

With that, everyone took a running start and leaped into the pile, leaves scattering in all directions as they landed. Ember's heart soared as he felt the soft crunch of leaves beneath him. Laughter filled the air, mixing with the rustle of leaves as his friends tumbled and rolled in the pile. They kicked up leaves, creating a whirlwind of colors around them, and Ember couldn't help but laugh along, feeling a joy deeper than he had ever imagined.

Hazel rolled onto her back, holding her belly as she laughed. "This is amazing, Ember! I've never jumped into such a big pile!"

LEO AND THE LEAF PILE

Midge, who had been fluttering around the pile, landed beside them, her feathers ruffled but her face glowing with delight. "It's even more fun than I thought it would be!" she chirped, tossing a few leaves into the air with her beak.

Thorn, the shy hedgehog, had also joined in, though he rolled carefully to avoid losing his little leaf umbrella. He giggled softly as he nestled into the pile, feeling the soft crunch of leaves around him. "I never thought I'd like this so much," he admitted shyly. "Thank you, Ember, for inviting me."

Ember beamed, feeling a warm sense of pride and contentment as he watched his friends enjoy the pile. It wasn't just his accomplishment anymore—it was a shared joy, something they had all made special together.

As they continued playing, Ember noticed Luna, the fox, hanging back near the edge of the pile. Luna was usually quite playful, but today she seemed hesitant, her eyes darting toward the pile with a look of longing. Ember approached her, curious.

"Luna, aren't you going to jump in?" he asked, nudging her gently with his paw.

Luna shuffled her feet, looking down. "Well... I'd love to," she admitted, "but I was worried about messing up the pile. You worked so hard on it, and I don't want to ruin it."

Ember's heart softened. "Oh, Luna, don't worry about that!" he reassured her. "This pile was made for everyone to enjoy, even if it gets a little messy. The more we play, the better it is!"

Luna's face brightened, and she gave Ember a grateful nod. She took a running leap, diving right into the center of the pile, leaves flying everywhere as she landed. Her laughter echoed through the valley, and Ember felt a deep sense of joy watching her finally let go and enjoy herself.

The friends continued playing, each one finding new ways to explore and enjoy the pile. Zinnia suggested they play a game where everyone had to hide in the leaves, and the last one found would be the winner. Ember loved the idea, and they all quickly buried themselves in the pile, giggling as they tried to keep still. It wasn't long before the pile was alive with the sound of muffled laughter, leaves shifting as everyone tried to stay hidden.

Fern, the chipmunk, who was very good at hiding, managed to stay hidden the longest. They cheered as she popped her head out from under a pile of leaves, grinning from ear to ear. "I think this is the best game ever!" she declared, and everyone agreed wholeheartedly.

Chapter 5: A Little Visitor

As the sun rose over the Valley of Echoes the next day, casting golden light through the trees, Ember stirred awake with a yawn. His leaf pile was now a scattered, colorful carpet around the big oak tree, remnants of the laughter and fun he'd shared with his friends. Ember smiled to himself as he stretched, remembering the way everyone had come together, bringing their unique spark to his grand creation.

Today, Ember planned to rebuild the pile. He wanted to surprise his friends by making it even bigger and fluffier than before. With a determined twinkle in his eye, Ember set off, collecting leaves once again, hopping from tree to tree as he filled his little basket with autumn's brightest treasures.

He was so absorbed in his work that he didn't notice a small set of eyes watching him from behind a thick bush. Pip, a young chipmunk with soft brown fur and a white stripe down his back, had been watching Ember for quite some time. Pip was shy by nature, often hiding in his cozy burrow, but he was deeply curious about the leaf pile that had become the talk of the valley.

Pip had heard from Hazel that Ember's pile was the biggest, fluffiest, most colorful leaf pile anyone had ever seen. The idea thrilled him, but he was also nervous. He had always been too shy to approach the older animals, and he wasn't sure if he'd be welcome.

After gathering a fresh batch of leaves, Ember noticed the quiet figure by the bush. He waved his paw, hoping to coax Pip out of hiding. "Hello there!" he called. "I see you over there. Would you like to help me with my leaf pile?"

Pip's eyes grew wide, and he took a hesitant step forward, unsure of what to say. He shuffled his paws nervously, his little heart pounding. "Oh, um... I don't know," he mumbled, his voice barely above a whisper. "I've never built a leaf pile before."

Ember gave him an encouraging smile. "That's okay! Neither had I when I started this one. Come on—why don't you help me gather some leaves? You'll be a natural!"

After a moment of hesitation, Pip nodded and scampered over to join Ember. Ember handed him a small bunch of leaves, and Pip took them carefully, his tiny paws trembling with excitement. Together, they worked side by side, collecting more leaves and rebuilding the pile. With each leaf they added, Pip grew a little braver, and a small smile appeared on his face.

As they worked, Ember noticed Pip's shy demeanor and decided to make him feel comfortable. "You know, Pip," he said kindly, "I used to be nervous about meeting new friends too. But building this pile has shown me that it's okay to feel shy. Everyone here is friendly and happy to welcome new friends."

Pip's face lit up at Ember's words. "Really? I thought maybe… maybe everyone wouldn't notice me or want me there."

Ember shook his head, placing a paw on Pip's shoulder. "Everyone is important, Pip. Sometimes, the smallest friends bring the brightest joy." He looked up as he noticed Hazel trotting over, her bushy tail bouncing as she approached.

Hazel stopped in front of them, her eyes bright with excitement. "Ember! You're making the pile even bigger today?" Then, she noticed Pip, who had taken a small step back, trying to hide behind a leaf. "Oh, hello, Pip! It's good to see you! Are you helping with the pile?"

Pip blushed and nodded shyly. "Y-yes, I am."

Hazel's face softened, and she gave him an encouraging smile. "I'm so glad you're here! It's always more fun with more friends." She grabbed a bunch of leaves and placed them at the base of the pile. "We can make it the biggest one yet, and then we can all jump together!"

Pip's eyes sparkled with excitement at the idea of joining in the fun. He had always wanted to be part of a group, to feel the thrill of playing

LEO AND THE LEAF PILE

alongside others. Encouraged by Hazel's friendly words, Pip worked harder, gathering leaves with renewed enthusiasm.

As they worked, more friends arrived, drawn by the news of Ember's growing pile. Bramble the hedgehog, Luna the fox, and Midge the magpie all joined in, each bringing their own special way of gathering leaves. The animals chatted and laughed, sharing stories as they worked, and Pip's nervousness began to melt away. He felt a sense of belonging he had never experienced before.

Soon, the pile was even taller than it had been before, reaching nearly twice Ember's height. It was the fluffiest, softest, most colorful pile any of them had ever seen, and Ember couldn't wait to jump into it with his friends.

With the pile ready, Ember looked around at his gathered friends. "Alright, everyone!" he called, raising a paw. "Let's all jump in together!"

The animals lined up, each one buzzing with excitement. Pip stood at the edge of the line, his paws trembling as he prepared for his first big leap. Ember noticed his nervousness and gave him an encouraging nod.

"Remember, Pip, we're all here together," Ember said gently. "Just take a deep breath, and jump when you're ready."

Pip nodded, taking a deep breath and gathering his courage. As Ember counted down, Pip closed his eyes, imagining the thrill of the jump, the softness of the leaves, and the joy of being surrounded by friends.

"One... two... THREE!" Ember shouted, and with a great cheer, they all leaped into the pile.

The moment Pip hit the leaves, he was surrounded by a flurry of colors and laughter. Leaves flew in every direction, and Pip found himself giggling as he tumbled through the soft, crunchy pile. The feeling was better than he had imagined—it was like diving into a sea of warmth, surrounded by the cheerful sounds of his friends.

As they continued to play, Ember noticed the joy on Pip's face. He saw how Pip's shyness had transformed into laughter and excitement. It warmed Ember's heart to see his new friend embracing the moment, fully enjoying the experience of sharing in the fun.

After they had all jumped several times, they settled into the leaves, catching their breath and basking in the warmth of the sun. Pip sat beside Ember, his face glowing with happiness.

"Thank you, Ember," Pip said softly, looking up at him with wide, grateful eyes. "I was so nervous to join, but... this is the best day I've ever had."

Ember smiled, feeling a sense of pride and joy. "I'm glad you came, Pip. Friends make everything better, and I'm lucky to have met you."

They sat together in comfortable silence, watching as the leaves around them shimmered in the sunlight. The pile was no longer just a collection of leaves—it was a place where friendships blossomed, where laughter echoed, and where everyone, no matter how big or small, found a place to belong

Chapter 6: The Leaf Dance

The following day, Ember awoke with a bright idea, one that filled him with excitement as he peeked outside his tree hollow. The leaf pile had been scattered and reshaped by their jumping, rolling, and games the day before, but to Ember, it still looked like a beautiful burst of color spread across the forest floor. This morning, he wanted to try something new—something that everyone could enjoy and that would bring fresh life to their leaf-filled fun.

As he hopped down to the ground, he noticed Pip, Hazel, and Midge already waiting near the pile. Their faces brightened when they saw him, eager to hear what he had in mind.

"Good morning, everyone!" Ember called, waving his paw cheerfully. "I had an idea I think you'll all enjoy."

Pip's eyes sparkled with curiosity. "What is it, Ember?"

"Well," Ember began, his tail flicking with excitement, "we've jumped, we've rolled, and we've hidden in the leaves. But what if we tried something we haven't done yet—like a leaf dance?"

Hazel tilted her head, her bushy tail swishing with interest. "A leaf dance? What's that?"

Ember grinned, his imagination sparking as he explained. "We can toss the leaves into the air, watch them float down, and move along with them! Imagine the leaves swirling around us, like a dance we make together. We'll all twirl and leap, matching the movement of the leaves."

Midge clapped her wings, her feathers ruffling with excitement. "That sounds wonderful, Ember! I love watching leaves float. It'll be like we're all part of the forest breeze!"

The friends nodded in agreement, their faces lighting up with enthusiasm. The idea of a leaf dance was new, but they were eager to give it a try.

As they gathered around the pile, Ember demonstrated how to start. "First, take a bunch of leaves in your paws," he instructed, "and toss them into the air. Then, we'll all move with the leaves, twirling, jumping, and swaying like they do."

With great enthusiasm, they each scooped up a handful of leaves. The moment Ember threw his leaves into the air, they all watched as the bright reds, oranges, and yellows floated gently down. Ember leaped up, twirling as he followed a leaf drifting toward the ground. Hazel hopped in circles, trying to catch a leaf on her nose, while Midge spread her wings, gliding gracefully as she moved with the leaves. Pip giggled as he spun in little circles, his eyes bright with joy as he watched the leaves flutter around him.

Before long, the friends were fully immersed in their leaf dance, moving with the colorful leaves as they floated through the air. The leaves seemed to dance with them, creating a magical scene that filled the valley with vibrant colors. They laughed as they twirled, each finding their own rhythm and movement.

As they danced, other animals in the valley began to notice the lively scene and wandered over to see what was happening. Zinnia, the playful rabbit, hopped closer, her nose twitching with curiosity. Fern, the chipmunk, and Luna, the fox, also came closer, their eyes wide with interest.

"What are you all doing?" Zinnia asked, her nose wiggling in excitement.

Ember paused, catching his breath as he explained. "We're doing a leaf dance! We throw the leaves up and move along with them, like we're part of the breeze."

Zinnia's eyes lit up, and she immediately grabbed a pawful of leaves, tossing them high into the air. "This looks like so much fun! I want to try too!"

One by one, the other animals joined in. Soon, the whole clearing was filled with friends, each throwing leaves into the air, laughing, and moving in their own unique way. Some, like Zinnia, bounced in quick, playful hops, while others, like Luna, moved in smooth, graceful leaps.

Thorn, the shy hedgehog, even took small, careful steps, swaying side to side as he watched the leaves float down around him.

The animals moved together, creating a dance that felt as natural as the autumn wind itself. The colors of the leaves blended with the movement of fur, feathers, and paws, forming a beautiful, swirling scene that filled the valley with life.

Ember watched his friends, his heart swelling with joy. He had wanted to create something new, but the leaf dance had become even more magical than he had imagined. Each friend brought their own style, and together, they created a unique, unspoken harmony that moved with the rhythm of the falling leaves.

After a while, Ember noticed Willow, the wise old owl, perched on a nearby branch, observing the dance with a warm, approving gaze. Her eyes sparkled as she watched the animals move together, and when Ember caught her eye, she gave him a nod of admiration.

"Your dance is beautiful, Ember," Willow called down, her voice carrying through the clearing. "It reminds me of the dances we used to have under the autumn moon many seasons ago. You've brought the forest to life with your creativity."

Ember's cheeks warmed at her praise, and he nodded gratefully. "Thank you, Willow! It's been wonderful seeing everyone enjoy the leaves together."

As the dance continued, Ember noticed that some of the animals had started pairing up, moving together in little duets. Hazel and Pip spun around, laughing as they tossed leaves back and forth to each other, while Luna and Fern created a game of catching the leaves before they hit the ground.

Feeling inspired, Ember reached out to Zinnia, who was twirling nearby. "Would you like to dance with me?" he asked, his eyes shining with excitement.

Zinnia grinned and grabbed his paw, and together, they spun through the leaves, laughter bubbling up as they moved. Each step felt light and joyful, and Ember felt a deep connection to his friend as they shared the moment, laughing and twirling together in the colorful flurry.

The leaf dance lasted until the sun was low in the sky, casting a warm, orange glow over the valley. Finally, they all came to a breathless stop, collapsing into the soft leaves as they caught their breath, their faces filled with smiles and their eyes shining with happiness.

As they lay in the scattered leaves, gazing up at the first stars twinkling in the sky, Ember felt a deep sense of gratitude for his friends. The leaf dance had brought them together in a way he hadn't anticipated, and the memory of their laughter and movement would stay with him for a long time.

Hazel sighed contentedly, resting her head on a pile of leaves. "This was the best day ever, Ember. I didn't know leaves could be so much fun!"

Midge nodded, her feathers still a bit ruffled from the dance. "It felt like we were all part of something bigger, like we were dancing with the whole forest."

Ember smiled, feeling his heart swell with happiness. "I'm so glad you all enjoyed it. I think we should make the leaf dance our tradition, something we do every autumn."

The friends murmured in agreement, each one eager to relive the joy they had shared. They all agreed that from now on, whenever the leaves fell and covered the valley, they would come together for a leaf dance, celebrating the season and their friendship.

Chapter 7: Bramble's Invitation

The morning sun cast a gentle glow over the Valley of Echoes, and the forest was calm and quiet, save for the occasional rustle of leaves in the breeze. After their magical leaf dance the day before, Ember was ready for a new adventure. As he made his way to the leaf pile, still partly scattered from the dance, he noticed that his friend Bramble, the hedgehog, was already there, carefully inspecting a pile of bright yellow leaves.

"Good morning, Bramble!" Ember called out as he trotted over. Bramble looked up, his small, round face lighting up with a warm smile.

"Good morning, Ember!" Bramble replied. "I thought I'd come by early to see if you needed help gathering more leaves."

Ember smiled, feeling grateful. "That sounds wonderful, Bramble! But you know, I was actually thinking about inviting some more friends to join us today. The leaf dance was so much fun, and I think there are others who would enjoy it too."

Bramble's eyes widened in delight. "That's a great idea, Ember! Who do you have in mind?"

"Well," Ember said thoughtfully, "there's a little mouse named Clover who lives near the riverbank. She's a bit shy, but I think she'd love to join us if we invite her. And there's Tumble, the young badger, who's been curious about our pile for a while."

Bramble nodded eagerly. "I think they'd both have a wonderful time. Let's go find them!"

The two friends set off, their excitement building as they went. First, they headed toward the riverbank, where they found Clover nibbling on a small berry near her burrow. The little mouse was startled at first when she saw them approaching, but Ember gave her a gentle smile, hoping to reassure her.

"Hello, Clover!" Ember greeted her warmly. "Bramble and I were wondering if you'd like to join us at the leaf pile. We're going to have some games and maybe another leaf dance."

Clover's whiskers twitched nervously, and she looked down at her tiny paws. "Oh, um... I don't know. I've never really played in a leaf pile before," she admitted shyly.

Ember stepped closer, his voice gentle. "You don't have to do anything you're not comfortable with. You can just sit with us, or watch the others if you like. We'd just love to have you there."

Clover's eyes softened, and a small smile spread across her face. "Alright, I'll come. It sounds like fun."

With Clover joining them, they set off to find Tumble, the young badger who lived near a large cluster of bushes. They found him happily rolling in the dirt, enjoying the early morning sun. Tumble looked up, his eyes brightening as he spotted Ember and Bramble.

"Hey, Ember! Bramble!" Tumble called, waddling over to them. "What brings you here so early?"

"We're inviting you to the leaf pile," Bramble explained, grinning. "We thought it would be fun if you came to play with us."

Tumble's face lit up with excitement. "A leaf pile? I've never jumped in one before! That sounds amazing! Count me in!"

With their new friends in tow, Ember, Bramble, Clover, and Tumble made their way back to the leaf pile, chatting and laughing along the way. When they arrived, they found that other animals, drawn by the excitement, had already gathered nearby, eager to see what new game Ember had planned.

As they reached the pile, Ember explained their first game. "Today, we're going to play a game called 'Leaf Maze!'" he announced, his eyes twinkling with anticipation. "We'll create paths and tunnels in the pile, and we'll try to find our way from one end to the other without peeking over the top. It'll be like a mini adventure through the leaves!"

The friends gasped with excitement, each one eager to explore this new game. Ember, Clover, Tumble, Bramble, and the others began reshaping the leaf pile, pushing and arranging leaves to create winding paths and little tunnels that crisscrossed through the center. They worked together, giggling and exchanging ideas, and before long, the pile had transformed into a colorful labyrinth.

When the maze was complete, they each took turns entering from one end and trying to find their way through to the other side. Clover, despite her initial nervousness, took her turn with a soft, determined smile, carefully stepping through the leaves as her friends cheered her on.

"Go, Clover! You're doing great!" Tumble called, his voice booming with encouragement.

Clover's eyes sparkled as she continued through the maze, and with a final leap, she emerged on the other side, greeted by cheers from everyone around. She looked at Ember with gratitude, her shyness melting away as she basked in the warmth of her friends' support.

"This is so much fun," she whispered to Ember. "Thank you for inviting me."

Ember gave her a gentle nudge. "I'm glad you're here, Clover. The games wouldn't be the same without you."

Tumble, with his boundless energy, made his way through the maze next, barreling through with gleeful abandon. Leaves flew in all directions as he stumbled and turned, eventually making his way to the end, laughing as he emerged.

After everyone had their turn, Ember suggested they try a different game. "How about we play 'Leaf Hide-and-Seek'?" he proposed, his face lighting up. "One of us will hide under the leaves, and the rest will try to find them. It'll be a new twist on hide-and-seek!"

The group cheered in agreement, and Bramble volunteered to be the first one to hide. He nestled himself into the leaves, curling up and covering himself completely. Once he was hidden, the others spread out, searching for little hints of movement or rustling.

Clover, who had become more confident with each game, moved quietly through the pile, her tiny ears listening for any sound that might give Bramble away. Suddenly, she spotted a small movement to her right—a tiny quiver of leaves—and she pounced, uncovering Bramble with a triumphant giggle.

"Got you, Bramble!" Clover cried, laughing as the others gathered around.

Bramble chuckled, shaking the leaves from his quills. "You're a great seeker, Clover! I didn't even see you coming!"

The group took turns hiding and seeking, each one adding their own twist to the game. Midge, with her keen eyes, proved to be an excellent seeker, while Tumble's playful enthusiasm made him a fun hider, often unable to stop giggling while waiting to be found.

As the games continued, Ember watched his friends, his heart swelling with happiness. Each friend had brought their own personality to the games, creating moments that were as unique as they were. The leaf pile, once a simple mound of autumn colors, had transformed into a space of laughter, encouragement, and friendship.

The animals were tired but content, their laughter filling the valley as they rested together in the leaves.

Ember gazed up the sky as he reflected on the day. It wasn't just the games that had made the day special, but the way each friend had come together, embracing each other's unique qualities and finding joy in their shared moments. He felt grateful for the friendships he had formed, and for the ways they had all supported and encouraged one another.

Chapter 8: An Unexpected Mess

The morning air was cool and crisp as Ember arrived at the leaf pile, ready for another day of games and fun with his friends. The early morning light filtered through the trees, casting a warm, golden glow over the Valley of Echoes. Ember felt excited to see what new adventures the day would bring, and he had an idea for a game that he couldn't wait to share with everyone.

One by one, his friends began to arrive. Clover, Pip, Hazel, Bramble, and Midge all joined him, their eyes bright with anticipation. Each of them had grown more comfortable in the leaf pile, and Ember loved watching how they embraced their playful sides.

"Good morning, everyone!" Ember greeted them with a big smile. "Today, I thought we could build little leaf nests in the pile. Each of us can create our own cozy spot to rest in!"

The group cheered in excitement, eagerly diving into the pile and collecting leaves to build their nests. Some gathered the biggest leaves they could find, while others layered soft, crinkly leaves to make their nests extra cozy. Bramble, with his small, careful paws, stacked leaves neatly, while Hazel playfully tossed leaves in every direction, her giggles echoing through the valley.

As they worked, the leaf pile became a flurry of activity. The friends chatted and laughed, each one focused on creating a unique nest. Ember smiled, feeling a warmth in his heart as he watched his friends build their own little spaces within the larger pile.

Suddenly, a strong gust of wind swept through the valley, sending leaves flying in every direction. Ember watched in surprise as their carefully constructed nests scattered, the wind blowing leaves high into the air. His friends gasped as the leaves they had so carefully gathered were torn away by the swirling breeze.

"Oh no!" Clover cried, reaching out in vain to catch a few of her leaves as they flew away.

Bramble looked around in dismay, his neatly arranged nest now a scattered mess. "All our hard work... it's all gone!" he said, his voice filled with disappointment.

Ember felt his heart sink as he saw the sadness on his friends' faces. They had all been so excited to build their nests, and now the wind had left the pile a mess. For a moment, no one spoke. The joy they had felt earlier seemed to have been swept away along with the leaves.

But Ember took a deep breath, determined to turn things around. He didn't want the day to end on a sad note. He looked at his friends with a gentle smile and said, "It's okay, everyone. We can rebuild our nests together. And who knows? Maybe we'll come up with something even better this time!"

Clover looked at Ember, her whiskers twitching uncertainly. "But it took us so long to make them," she said softly. "What if the wind just comes and blows them away again?"

Ember thought for a moment, then nodded. "You're right, Clover. The wind might blow again. But if we all work together, we can make our nests stronger. And even if the wind does come, we'll still have each other to help put things back together."

The friends exchanged glances, their spirits beginning to lift as they realized Ember was right. Working together had always made things more fun, and this time would be no different.

Ember stepped forward, scooping up a handful of leaves. "Let's start by gathering the leaves that blew away. If we each take a section, we'll have everything back in no time!"

Encouraged by Ember's words, the friends spread out, collecting leaves from every corner of the clearing. They laughed as they darted around, gathering colorful piles and placing them back in the center. Ember felt his heart swell with pride as he watched everyone working together, their laughter filling the air once again.

As they gathered leaves, they came up with a new plan for their nests. This time, they would build a big, shared nest in the middle of the pile—a cozy spot where everyone could fit, creating a space they could all enjoy together.

Bramble, always thoughtful and careful, suggested, "Maybe we could stack the leaves in layers, so the wind won't blow them away as easily."

Hazel nodded enthusiastically, her tail swishing with excitement. "And we could use some sticks to anchor the leaves in place. That way, if the wind comes again, they'll stay together!"

Ember smiled, feeling a rush of excitement as everyone contributed their ideas. "I love it! Let's make this nest the coziest, sturdiest one yet!"

The friends worked together, layering leaves and arranging sticks around the edges to secure their creation. They each added a personal touch to the shared nest—Clover brought some soft, downy feathers she had found, while Midge added a few colorful pebbles for decoration. Bramble, ever resourceful, gathered acorn caps to line the inside, making the nest feel even more inviting.

As they built, they shared stories and jokes, their laughter weaving through the leaves. The nest grew bigger and sturdier, each layer holding firm as they worked side by side. Ember felt a deep sense of satisfaction, knowing they had created something stronger together than they could have on their own.

When the nest was complete, the friends stood back to admire their work. It was cozy, inviting, and full of unique touches from each of them. Ember beamed, his heart filled with pride and joy.

"Great job, everyone!" he said, his voice full of warmth. "This nest is even better than the ones we started with. And the best part is that we made it together."

The friends gathered around the nest, settling in for a rest. As they rested, a gentle breeze stirred the air. This time, however, the nest held strong, and they all felt a wave of contentment knowing they had created something that could withstand the wind.

Clover sighed happily, snuggling deeper into the leaves. "I'm glad we didn't give up," she said softly. "If we had, we wouldn't have made this wonderful nest."

Ember nodded, looking at each of his friends with gratitude. "It's amazing what we can do when we work together. Even when things don't go as planned, we always have each other to make things better."

They lay in comfortable silence, watching the leaves sway gently above them as they drifted down from the trees. The day had started with an unexpected mess, but they had turned it into something beautiful by working together and supporting one another.

Chapter 9: The Leaf Game Rules

The next morning, Ember was eager to see his friends again. He felt a sense of excitement as he made his way to the shared nest they had built together in the leaf pile. The sturdiness of their work and the joy they'd found in working as a team had left a warmth in his heart that still lingered. He couldn't wait to see what new games and adventures the day would bring.

As he approached the clearing, he found that many of his friends were already there. Bramble, Clover, Hazel, and Pip were snuggled comfortably in the large nest, chatting and laughing. Midge, with her sharp eye for detail, was rearranging a few of the acorn caps they had used for decoration, making the nest feel even cozier.

"Good morning, everyone!" Ember called out, waving a paw as he trotted over to join them.

"Good morning, Ember!" the friends chorused, their faces lighting up as he arrived. They were all eager to start the day, and the energy in the air was contagious.

Ember sat down in the nest, looking around at his friends with a smile. "I thought we could come up with a new game to play today," he suggested. "Something that's fun for everyone."

The friends nodded in agreement, their eyes shining with excitement.

Clover, who had become more confident with each passing day, piped up. "How about a game where we all take turns jumping into the nest from different spots around the pile? We could call it 'Nest Jump!'"

The friends murmured in approval, and Ember smiled. "That sounds like a great idea, Clover! But let's make sure we all play safely and fairly so that everyone can enjoy the game."

Bramble nodded thoughtfully. "Maybe we should make a few rules so that everyone knows how to play," he suggested. "That way, no one gets hurt, and everyone has a turn."

Ember agreed, and the friends began brainstorming rules for their new game. They wanted to make sure it was fair and fun, with everyone having an equal chance to participate.

After a few minutes of discussion, they came up with the following rules:

1. Each friend would take turns jumping into the nest, one at a time, to ensure everyone had enough space.
2. They would choose a "start spot" for each jump so that no one took too big of a leap, which could lead to bumps and spills.
3. Everyone would cheer for each jumper, encouraging each friend to have fun, no matter how big or small their jump.
4. If anyone felt nervous or wanted to skip their turn, they could sit out without any pressure. The game was about fun, not competition.
5. To keep things fair, each friend would go in order and wait until everyone had had a turn before jumping again.

As they finished creating their rules, Ember felt a warm sense of pride in his friends. They had thought carefully about making sure the game was enjoyable for everyone, and he loved seeing how much they cared for one another.

"All right, everyone!" Ember announced with a grin. "Now that we have our rules, let's play 'Nest Jump!' Who wants to go first?"

Hazel's paw shot up instantly, her eyes gleaming with excitement. "I'll go first! I love jumping!"

The friends cheered for her as she positioned herself at the first "start spot," a soft patch of ground a few steps away from the nest. With a joyful bound, she leaped into the air, landing softly in the middle of the nest with a big smile on her face.

"That was amazing, Hazel!" Bramble cheered, clapping his tiny paws together.

One by one, the friends took turns jumping into the nest, each one adding their own style to the game. Midge, who had a flair for grace, spread her wings as she jumped, fluttering gently down like a leaf drifting on the breeze. Pip, with his small, shy nature, took a careful hop, his face lighting up as he landed safely in the nest.

When it was Bramble's turn, he chose to do a little spin as he jumped, his quills swishing in the air as he landed. The friends clapped and laughed, celebrating each unique jump, and Ember felt his heart swell with happiness as he watched them all having so much fun.

As the game continued, Ember noticed that each friend brought something special to their jump. Hazel's jumps were big and bold, while Clover's were small and gentle. Midge's jumps were elegant, and Pip's were careful but filled with a quiet joy. Each jump was a reflection of their unique personalities, and Ember felt a deep appreciation for the different ways they each added to the group's fun.

After a few rounds, Ember noticed Clover hesitating at her start spot. She shuffled her paws, glancing nervously at the nest.

"What's wrong, Clover?" Ember asked gently, sensing her uncertainty.

Clover looked down, her ears drooping slightly. "I... I want to try a bigger jump, but I'm a little scared," she admitted softly. "What if I don't make it all the way to the nest?"

Ember gave her a reassuring smile. "You can do it, Clover. But remember, you don't have to do anything that makes you uncomfortable. We're here to have fun together."

The friends nodded in agreement, offering her warm smiles and encouraging words. Feeling a little braver, Clover took a deep breath, then gave a tiny hop that was a bit bigger than her usual jumps. She landed in the nest, her face glowing with pride as her friends cheered for her.

"You did great, Clover!" Hazel said, giving her a gentle nudge. "It was a perfect jump!"

As they continued the game, Ember felt a sense of unity among the group. They supported each other, cheered each other on, and celebrated every small accomplishment, making sure each friend felt valued and included. The rules they had created weren't just about keeping the game safe—they were about fostering a spirit of kindness, respect, and encouragement.

When it was Ember's turn again, he decided to try something new. He hopped up onto a nearby rock, giving him a bit more height. He took a deep breath, then leaped off the rock and into the nest, landing in a flurry of leaves. His friends burst into laughter and applause, and Ember grinned, feeling a thrill of excitement.

"Great jump, Ember!" Midge chirped, clapping her wings together. "That was fantastic!"

They continued playing until dusk. By then, they were all tired but happy, their hearts full from a day of laughter and friendship.

Chapter 10: A Surprise for Nettle

The morning sun shone brightly over the Valley of Echoes, casting a golden light over the forest as Ember hurried to the leaf pile. Today felt special, though he couldn't quite explain why. The leaf pile, now a cozy nest layered with days of memories, seemed to glow with the warmth of all the laughter, games, and friendships it had gathered.

As he reached the clearing, he found his friends already there. Hazel, Clover, Bramble, and Midge were chatting and laughing, clearly just as excited for the new day as he was. Each of them wore smiles, their faces alight with anticipation.

"Good morning, everyone!" Ember greeted, waving a paw.

"Good morning, Ember!" his friends called back, their voices ringing cheerfully through the clearing.

As they settled into the leaf pile, enjoying the fresh morning breeze, they noticed a figure lurking just beyond the trees. It was Nettle, the young fox cub who had recently moved to the Valley of Echoes with her family. Though Nettle was friendly, she was shy, and she often preferred watching from a distance rather than joining in the games. The others hadn't seen much of her since she arrived in the valley, but Ember had always thought she seemed curious and kind.

Hazel noticed her first, nudging Ember and whispering, "Isn't that Nettle over there? I wonder if she wants to join us."

Ember nodded thoughtfully. "I think she does, but maybe she's a bit too shy to ask." He looked at his friends with a gentle smile. "What if we invite her to play with us today? I bet she'd love it, and it would be nice to help her feel more at home here."

The friends nodded in agreement, each of them eager to welcome Nettle and make her feel like part of the group. They had all experienced moments of shyness or uncertainty, and they knew how much a friendly invitation could mean.

Ember waved to Nettle, calling out to her with a warm smile. "Hi, Nettle! Would you like to come and join us?"

Nettle hesitated, her amber eyes widening as she glanced around the clearing. She shuffled her paws, looking unsure, but after a moment, she gave a small nod and trotted over, her tail flicking nervously behind her.

"Hi, everyone," she said softly, her voice barely a whisper as she glanced shyly at the group.

"Welcome, Nettle!" Clover said brightly, giving her a friendly smile. "We're so glad you came!"

The friends all welcomed her with warmth, and Ember could see Nettle's nervousness melting away. She looked a bit more comfortable now, her tail swishing in small, happy movements.

"Thank you for inviting me," Nettle murmured, glancing shyly at Ember. "I've always wanted to play with everyone, but I didn't know if... well, if it was okay."

Ember's heart softened. "You're always welcome with us, Nettle. We love making new friends, and we'd be happy to have you join our games."

Nettle's face lit up, her shyness replaced with a hopeful smile. The friends gathered closer, eager to include her in their plans for the day. They decided to play one of their favorite games, "Leaf Tag," where each friend had to tag another using a leaf rather than their paw. It was a gentle, playful way to keep everyone safe and make sure no one felt left out.

Ember explained the rules to Nettle, who listened carefully, her eyes bright with excitement. She picked up a golden leaf, holding it carefully in her paws as she prepared to join the game.

The game began, and the friends darted around the clearing, laughing and tossing leaves as they tried to tag each other. Hazel leaped gracefully over the nest, her eyes gleaming as she tagged Clover with a soft, crinkly red leaf. Bramble scurried around, using his small size to dart between the others, while Midge glided above, diving down with leaves and tagging her friends from the air.

Nettle joined in with growing confidence, her shyness fading as she became more immersed in the game. She tagged Pip with a leaf, her laughter echoing through the valley as she darted away, enjoying the freedom of play. Ember felt a surge of happiness as he watched her, thrilled to see her joy blossom.

After a while, they all collapsed into the nest, breathless and laughing, their faces flushed with happiness.

"That was so much fun!" Nettle exclaimed, her eyes bright with excitement. "Thank you for letting me play with you."

Ember reached over and gave her a gentle nudge. "We're so glad you joined us, Nettle. You made the game even more fun!"

As they rested, Ember thought of a way to make the day even more special for Nettle. He wanted her to feel truly welcome, and he knew just the thing to make her feel appreciated.

"Why don't we give Nettle a special title for the day?" Ember suggested, his eyes twinkling with mischief. "How about we make her the 'Leaf Champion' of the Valley of Echoes?"

The friends cheered, loving the idea. Nettle's eyes widened with surprise, and her cheeks flushed with delight.

"Oh, really?" she stammered, her voice filled with wonder. "I've never been the champion of anything before."

Ember grinned and nodded. "You're the Leaf Champion for today, Nettle! We'll make you a special crown from the leaves we've gathered, and you can lead us in our games."

The friends immediately began gathering the most beautiful leaves they could find, selecting vibrant reds, golds, and oranges to make Nettle's crown. Bramble found some acorn caps, which he wove into the crown for an added touch, while Midge picked up a few tiny wildflowers to decorate it further.

When they finished, Ember placed the crown on Nettle's head, stepping back to admire their work. Nettle's face glowed with happiness as she looked at each of her friends, clearly touched by their gesture.

"Thank you, everyone," she whispered, her voice full of emotion. "I feel so special... like I truly belong here."

"You do belong here, Nettle," Hazel said warmly. "You're our friend, and we're so glad you're with us."

The friends gathered around her, each of them feeling the warmth of their bond. They had come together, welcoming Nettle into their group with open hearts, and the moment felt magical.

With her new crown, Nettle led them in a game she called "Leaf Hunt," where they had to search the clearing for leaves of specific colors. She would call out a color, and everyone would scatter, searching for the leaf that matched. It was a game that combined fun and teamwork, as the friends worked together to find every leaf.

"Red!" Nettle called, and the friends darted off, looking for the brightest red leaf they could find. Clover returned first, her paws clasping a scarlet leaf that seemed to glow in the sunlight.

"Good job, Clover!" Nettle said, her voice full of encouragement.

They continued playing, each friend bringing back leaves of different colors, from golden yellows to deep purples. The game brought laughter and smiles, and Nettle's confidence grew with each round. She had found her place in the group, her joy shining brightly as she led her friends.

Chapter 11: The Best Jump Contest

The sun rose over the Valley of Echoes, casting a soft, golden light through the trees as Ember made his way to the leaf pile. Today, he felt a special excitement buzzing in the air. His friends had all been talking about ways to challenge themselves, pushing the limits of their games and coming up with new ideas for fun. Ember couldn't wait to see what creative challenges his friends would bring to the day.

As he approached the clearing, he saw that his friends had already gathered. Hazel, Clover, Bramble, Midge, Pip, and even Nettle stood near the leaf pile, each one looking eager and energized. They chatted among themselves, laughing and sharing ideas, and Ember felt his heart swell with happiness. It was moments like these that reminded him how much their little community had grown, thanks to the leaf pile that had brought them all together.

"Good morning, everyone!" Ember called, waving as he joined them.

"Good morning, Ember!" they all replied, their faces lighting up with excitement.

Once they were all settled, Hazel spoke up. "I had an idea last night," she said, her tail flicking with enthusiasm. "What if we have a contest to see who can make the best jump into the leaf pile? We could each try to make our jump special, like adding a twist or doing a spin."

The friends murmured in agreement, their eyes sparkling with interest. Hazel's idea sounded thrilling, and everyone was eager to give it a try.

Ember nodded, smiling at his friend. "That's a great idea, Hazel! We'll each take a turn and do our best jump, and we can all cheer each other on."

Midge tilted her head, adding thoughtfully, "Maybe we could even give each other some friendly feedback. That way, we can all improve and try new things."

The group nodded in agreement, loving the idea of learning from each other and growing together. The contest wasn't about winning or being the best—it was about having fun, learning new skills, and encouraging each other to reach their full potential.

They decided to set a few simple rules:

1. Each friend would get one turn to jump, and they could choose any style they wanted.
2. After each jump, everyone would offer positive feedback and suggestions to make it even better.
3. The most important rule was to have fun and celebrate each jump, no matter how big or small.

With the rules agreed upon, Ember looked around at his friends. "Who wants to go first?"

Pip raised his paw shyly. "I'll go first," he offered, his voice soft but determined. Pip was known for his careful, precise nature, and though he was shy, he loved to challenge himself in new ways.

The friends cheered for him as he positioned himself a few steps from the leaf pile, taking a deep breath to steady his nerves. With a small smile, he took a running start, then leaped gracefully into the pile, landing with a soft crunch in the center. Though his jump was simple, Pip's elegance and care shone through, and the friends clapped, beaming with admiration.

"That was wonderful, Pip!" Clover said, her voice warm with encouragement. "You looked so graceful when you jumped!"

Hazel nodded, her eyes bright. "Maybe next time, you could try adding a little spin. I bet it would look amazing with your jump!"

Pip's cheeks flushed with pride, and he nodded, feeling encouraged by his friends' support. He had never thought to add a spin, but the idea filled him with excitement. He felt ready to try it next time, knowing his friends believed in him.

Next up was Bramble. Known for his careful, methodical nature, Bramble took a few moments to prepare, thinking through his jump before starting. He took a running leap, then curled into a little ball, landing in the pile with a playful roll that sent leaves scattering everywhere.

The friends laughed and clapped, delighted by Bramble's unique style.

"That was so creative, Bramble!" Midge chirped, clapping her wings together. "You looked like a little tumbleweed rolling through the leaves!"

Clover added, "Maybe next time, you could uncurl at the end and land with your paws out. It would make your jump look even bigger!"

Bramble grinned, nodding eagerly. He loved the idea of expanding his jump, and he felt grateful for the support and ideas his friends offered.

One by one, the friends took their turns. Midge, with her love of flight, spread her wings and glided down, doing a little twirl mid-air before landing softly. Her elegance and control earned cheers from everyone, and Hazel suggested she try a double twirl next time for even more flair.

When it was Clover's turn, she hopped lightly into the pile, her tiny paws barely disturbing the leaves. Though her jump was gentle, it was full of charm, and the friends encouraged her to add a little hop before she jumped to give it more bounce.

Finally, it was Hazel's turn. She was known for her bold and energetic nature, and her jumps were always lively. She took a big, enthusiastic leap, kicking her legs out as she soared through the air, landing with a delighted laugh in the center of the pile.

"That was fantastic, Hazel!" Ember said, clapping his paws together. "You have so much energy in your jump—it's like you're flying!"

Hazel grinned, her eyes gleaming with excitement. "Thank you, Ember! Maybe next time, I'll try adding a flip!"

With each jump, the friends offered kind words and suggestions, cheering each other on and celebrating each unique style. They were learning from each other, exploring new ways to jump, and having more fun than they'd ever imagined.

Finally, it was Ember's turn. He positioned himself at the edge of the clearing, taking a deep breath as he prepared to make his jump. He thought back to all the wonderful jumps he'd seen from his friends, drawing inspiration from each one.

With a smile, he took a running start, then leaped high into the air. As he reached the peak of his jump, he twisted his body, doing a full spin before landing in the leaf pile with a joyful laugh. The friends burst into applause, their cheers filling the valley as they celebrated his jump.

"That was amazing, Ember!" Nettle said, her face full of admiration. "You looked so confident up there!"

Ember grinned, feeling a warmth in his chest. "Thank you, Nettle! I was inspired by all of you. Each of your jumps showed me something new, and I wanted to try combining them."

The friends gathered around, their hearts full as they shared their thoughts and ideas. They had each brought something special to the game, and they felt a deep sense of pride in the unique skills they had shared.

Ember gathered his friends close. "I'm so proud of each of you," he said softly. "Today wasn't just about jumping—it was about learning from each other and celebrating what makes each of us special."

The friends shook their heads, their faces filled with contentment. They had learned that true friendship was about more than games; it was about lifting each other up, sharing new ideas, and encouraging one another to be their best selves.

Chapter 12: A Little Visitor

It was a crisp, cool morning in the Valley of Echoes, and Ember felt a renewed excitement as he made his way to the leaf pile. Each day, he looked forward to meeting his friends, sharing laughter, games, and the warmth of their growing friendship. As he approached the clearing, he noticed that his friends were already gathered around, chatting happily and sharing ideas for the day's games.

"Good morning, everyone!" Ember called, waving his paw.

"Good morning, Ember!" his friends chorused back, their faces lighting up with smiles.

As they settled into the leaf pile, Ember noticed a little movement near the edge of the clearing. Peeking out from behind a tree was a tiny creature with soft gray fur, large eyes, and a pair of twitching whiskers. It was a young mouse named Willow, a newcomer to the valley who had recently arrived with her family. Willow had been a bit shy, often staying close to her family's burrow, but Ember had noticed her watching the games from afar, clearly curious about the group.

Ember's heart went out to her; he remembered when he had felt shy and uncertain around new friends, and he wanted Willow to feel as welcome as he had. He waved to her with a warm smile. "Hello, Willow!" he called out. "Would you like to come and join us?"

Willow's eyes widened with surprise, and she shuffled her paws, looking uncertain. She cast a glance at the leaf pile and then back at Ember, clearly tempted but unsure.

The friends noticed her hesitation, and Clover stepped forward, her gentle voice filled with kindness. "You're more than welcome to join us, Willow. We're just about to play a new game, and it would be wonderful to have you with us."

Willow took a small step forward, her whiskers twitching nervously. "Thank you," she said softly, her voice barely a whisper. "I've... I've never played in a leaf pile before."

Hazel smiled warmly, her eyes full of encouragement. "Well, today is the perfect day to try it out! We'll show you all the fun things we can do with the leaves."

With a little more courage, Willow took another step forward, moving closer to the group. Ember felt a warm sense of happiness as he saw his friends making her feel at ease. They had all experienced moments of shyness, and they knew how much a friendly invitation could mean.

Once Willow had joined the circle, Ember explained the game they were going to play. "Today, we're going to play 'Leaf Castle!'" he said, his voice full of excitement. "We'll each build our own mini castle out of leaves, twigs, and anything else we can find around the clearing. When we're done, we'll share our castles with each other."

Willow's eyes sparkled with curiosity. "That sounds... amazing," she whispered, a small smile forming on her face.

The friends immediately set to work, each of them gathering leaves, twigs, and other small treasures to build their castles. Willow moved carefully, choosing each leaf and twig with great care, her tiny paws trembling slightly as she placed each piece. Ember stayed nearby, occasionally giving her a gentle smile or offering a word of encouragement.

Hazel, ever the imaginative one, built her castle with walls made of crinkly red leaves, while Bramble constructed a cozy, rounded structure using layers of soft golden leaves. Clover made a tiny tower with her twigs, adding a delicate crown of acorn caps at the top. Ember decided to use a mix of colors for his castle, creating a bright and vibrant fortress.

Willow worked quietly, her small face set in concentration. She placed each leaf with care, building a tiny castle that looked more like a cozy nest. She used soft leaves for the walls and added tiny pebbles around the base for decoration. It was a simple, beautiful structure, and her friends admired her attention to detail.

When the castles were complete, the friends gathered around to share their creations. Each castle was unique, reflecting its creator's personality and style. They admired one another's work, offering kind words and encouragement.

As they came to Willow's castle, her face turned a little red, and she looked down shyly. "It's... it's not as big as the others," she mumbled, her voice barely audible.

Ember knelt down beside her castle, his eyes full of admiration. "It may be small, but it's beautiful, Willow. You've put so much care into it, and that makes it special."

The friends nodded in agreement, each of them expressing their appreciation for her castle. Willow's face brightened, her initial shyness giving way to a look of pride and happiness.

Hazel reached over and gave Willow's castle a gentle pat. "I think it's perfect, Willow. It looks cozy, just like you!"

With her newfound confidence, Willow smiled, her heart filled with warmth from the kindness of her friends. She looked at her castle with pride, feeling a sense of belonging she had never felt before.

As the friends played near the leaf pile, Ember noticed that Willow seemed to be opening up more. She laughed along with the others, her shyness melting away as she became more comfortable. She even suggested a new game, one where they had to hide tiny treasures in their castles and challenge each other to find them.

The friends loved the idea, and they each hid small objects—pebbles, tiny pinecones, and bits of bark—within their castles. Then they took turns searching each castle to find the hidden treasures, laughing as they uncovered each carefully concealed item. Willow's castle, with its cozy walls and soft leaves, proved to be a tricky one, and her friends marveled at her clever hiding spots.

Throughout the game, Ember felt a deep sense of joy watching Willow come out of her shell. She was no longer the quiet observer on the edge of the clearing—she was now a full part of the group, laughing, playing, and sharing her ideas. Her friends had welcomed her with open hearts, and in return, she had brought a gentle, creative spirit that enriched their games and added a new layer of warmth to their friendship.

As the day wore on, the friends gathered in the leaf pile to rest. They chatted and shared stories, their laughter filling the air as they enjoyed each other's company.

Willow nestled into the pile beside Clover, her eyes filled with gratitude. "Thank you, everyone," she said softly, her voice warm with emotion. "I was so nervous to join, but... today has been one of the happiest days of my life. I've never felt so welcome."

Ember gave her a gentle nudge, his face full of kindness. "You're one of us now, Willow. We're so glad you're here with us."

They all murmured in agreement, each of them feeling the joy that came from including Willow in their group. They had learned that friendship was about more than just games—it was about making space for others, showing kindness, and creating an environment where everyone felt valued.

Chapter 13: A Lost Leaf

The morning in the Valley of Echoes was crisp and fresh as Ember arrived at the leaf pile. Today, he felt a sense of adventure buzzing in the air. Over the past days, he and his friends had shared laughter, games, and memories that had drawn them closer together, and Ember looked forward to the new stories they'd create today.

As he reached the clearing, he noticed his friends gathering, their eyes bright with anticipation. Bramble, Clover, Hazel, Midge, Pip, Nettle, and even Willow were all present, chatting happily as they waited for the day's adventures to begin.

"Good morning, everyone!" Ember called, waving his paw with a cheerful smile.

"Good morning, Ember!" they replied, their faces lighting up.

Ember joined the group, settling into the familiar comfort of the leaf pile. As they discussed ideas for the day, Midge fluttered over, her wings gleaming in the morning sun. She wore a beautiful, iridescent leaf tucked into her feathers, the colors shimmering in shades of green, blue, and silver.

"Midge, that leaf is beautiful!" Hazel exclaimed, her eyes widening in admiration. "Where did you find it?"

Midge's eyes sparkled as she explained, "I found it near the riverbank yesterday. I've never seen a leaf like it before, and I thought it would be perfect to wear today."

The friends gathered closer, admiring the leaf. It was delicate and vibrant, with tiny sparkles of dew that caught the sunlight, making it look almost magical. Midge wore it proudly, feeling special with her unique little accessory.

As they began planning their games, Midge decided to take a short flight to find some twigs and pebbles for a new game they'd thought up. She spread her wings, flying in graceful circles above the clearing, her leaf shimmering as it caught the light. But as she dipped lower to land, a sudden gust of wind swept through the valley, catching her off guard. She fluttered wildly, trying to steady herself, but in the midst of the commotion, the shimmering leaf slipped from her feathers and was swept away by the breeze.

"Oh no!" Midge gasped, watching in dismay as her special leaf drifted away.

The friends noticed her distress and immediately gathered around, concern filling their faces. "What happened, Midge?" Ember asked gently.

"My leaf... it was my favorite leaf, and now it's gone!" Midge said softly, her voice tinged with sadness. "I looked everywhere yesterday to find it, and now it's lost."

Ember felt a pang of sympathy, knowing how much Midge had loved that leaf. He looked at his friends, each one of them sharing the same determined expression. "Don't worry, Midge. We'll help you find it! If we all look together, we're sure to spot it."

The friends nodded in agreement, each of them eager to help. Midge's leaf had brought a special sparkle to their day, and they wanted to do whatever they could to bring it back to her.

"We'll search the whole clearing and beyond," Clover suggested, her eyes filled with determination. "If it's out there, we'll find it!"

Encouraged by their words, Midge's face brightened. She felt grateful for their support, and her heart filled with hope. "Thank you, everyone. It means so much to me."

The friends spread out, each taking a section of the valley to search. Ember went toward the oak trees on the western side, where leaves often gathered in clusters. Bramble carefully searched around the base of the leaf pile, turning over leaves and twigs in case the wind had blown Midge's leaf into the crevices. Hazel and Pip scoured the area near the riverbank, their eyes scanning every nook and cranny.

Willow, who had a keen eye for detail, looked carefully among the patches of grass and rocks, hoping to catch a glimpse of the shimmering leaf. Nettle used her nose, sniffing the air in case she could pick up the scent of the river dew that had clung to Midge's leaf.

As they searched, Ember noticed how focused and determined each friend was. They were doing everything they could to help Midge, their kindness and friendship shining through with every step they took.

After a while, they gathered back in the clearing, each friend reporting what they had found. Ember looked at Midge, his voice filled with reassurance. "We may not have found it yet, but we're not giving up. We'll keep looking, and we'll find that leaf together."

Midge smiled, feeling encouraged by their unwavering support. Just knowing that her friends cared so much made the loss of her leaf a little easier to bear.

Suddenly, Willow perked up, her eyes lighting up with excitement. "I think I remember seeing something shiny near the big rock by the river!" she exclaimed. "It might have been your leaf, Midge. Let's go check it out!"

The group eagerly followed Willow, each one of them filled with hope. They arrived at the riverbank, where a large rock jutted out from the water's edge, casting a small shadow over the area. The friends spread out, their eyes scanning every leaf, twig, and pebble around the rock.

After a few moments, Hazel's voice rang out, "I found something!"

The friends rushed over, and there, wedged between two small stones, was Midge's leaf, still shimmering with its iridescent colors. The friends cheered, their voices echoing through the valley, and Midge's face lit up with joy as she carefully picked up her treasured leaf.

"Oh, thank you, everyone!" Midge cried, her voice filled with gratitude. "I couldn't have found it without you."

Ember gave her a gentle pat on the back, his face full of warmth. "That's what friends are for, Midge. We're always here to help each other."

As they made their way back to the clearing, the friends chatted happily, their spirits lifted by their success. Midge tucked her leaf safely into her feathers, promising to keep it close and secure.

Once they reached the leaf pile, Ember suggested they celebrate with a game. "How about we play 'Leaf Treasure Hunt'?" he proposed. "We can each hide a small object, and everyone else will search for it, just like we did with Midge's leaf."

The friends agreed eagerly, excited to put their new treasure-hunting skills to use. Each one of them chose a small object—a pebble, a twig, an acorn, or a colorful leaf—and hid it somewhere in the clearing. They took turns searching, laughing and cheering as they found each hidden item.

The game filled the air with joy, and as they played, Ember felt a deep sense of happiness watching his friends enjoy themselves. Midge's lost leaf had turned into an adventure, bringing them closer together and reminding them of the strength of their bond.

Chapter 14: The Leaf Lantern Idea

A gentle autumn breeze blew through the Valley of Echoes as Ember made his way to the leaf pile, the early morning light filtering softly through the trees. Today, he had a spark of inspiration for something new—a way to make their beloved leaf pile even more magical and inviting for everyone. He couldn't wait to share the idea with his friends and see what they would create together.

As he reached the clearing, he found that his friends were already gathered around the pile, chatting and laughing as they waited for him. Each face was bright with excitement, and Ember felt his heart swell with happiness at the sight.

"Good morning, everyone!" Ember called, waving a paw as he joined them.

"Good morning, Ember!" his friends chimed back, their voices filled with warmth.

After they all settled into the leaf pile, Ember cleared his throat, feeling a spark of anticipation. "I had an idea for something new we could make together," he began, his eyes twinkling. "What if we created a 'Leaf Lantern'?"

The friends exchanged curious glances, intrigued by the idea. "What's a Leaf Lantern?" asked Bramble, tilting his head in interest.

"Well," Ember explained, "we could build a lantern structure out of sticks, leaves, and anything else we can find. Then, as the sun begins to set, we could place a few fireflies inside to light it up. It would make the leaf pile glow in the evening, and we could all sit around it and enjoy the warm light together."

The friends gasped, their faces lighting up with excitement. The idea of a Leaf Lantern—a glowing, cozy light that would make their gathering space even more magical—filled them with joy.

"Oh, that sounds beautiful!" Clover said, her voice filled with wonder. "I've always loved watching fireflies at night. This would make it feel like a celebration!"

Hazel's eyes sparkled as she clapped her paws together. "Let's do it! We could each add something special to make the lantern unique."

With a cheer, the friends began to gather materials, their excitement building as they set to work on their shared creation. Ember led the way, finding sticks that would form the sturdy frame of the lantern. He selected thin, flexible branches that could be bent into a round shape, and Hazel helped him bind them together with vines to create a strong foundation.

Bramble, ever meticulous, gathered leaves of various colors and textures. He chose large, golden oak leaves and soft, red maple leaves, carefully layering them along the sides of the frame to form the lantern's walls. Clover added her own touch, tucking small acorn caps into the vines, creating a delicate border that added charm to the structure.

Willow, who had a keen eye for detail, found some feathers near the riverbank. She gently placed them between the leaves, their soft, fluffy tips peeking out, giving the lantern a whimsical look.

As they worked, each friend shared their ideas, and the lantern began to take on a unique character, reflecting the creativity and care of everyone involved.

Midge, who loved to add a little sparkle, brought over a few dewdrop-covered leaves she had found near the base of an old tree. "These dew-covered leaves will catch the light," she explained, tucking them between the others. "When the fireflies glow, the drops will make the light shimmer!"

The friends murmured in admiration, each one adding their own special touch. Nettle, who loved the scent of pine, brought over a few sprigs from a nearby tree and wove them into the lantern's structure. Their fresh scent filled the air, adding a comforting, earthy fragrance to the lantern.

As they worked, they chatted and laughed, sharing stories and ideas. The Leaf Lantern was becoming more than just a project—it was a collective expression of their friendship, filled with pieces of each friend's unique personality and creativity.

When the structure was complete, Ember stood back to admire their work. The lantern was round and sturdy, its walls covered in layers of colorful leaves, acorn caps, and delicate feathers. Dew-dappled leaves sparkled among the others, and the sprigs of pine added a lovely touch of green.

"It's beautiful," Ember said softly, his voice filled with awe. "You all did such an amazing job."

The friends looked at each other, their faces glowing with pride and happiness. Each of them had poured their hearts into the lantern, and the result was a work of art that reflected the warmth and kindness of their friendship.

With the sun beginning to dip lower in the sky, they decided it was time to gather fireflies for the lantern. Midge, being the quickest, offered to lead the way, and the friends followed her through the valley as they searched for the tiny, glowing insects.

They soon found a group of fireflies near a cluster of tall grass, their little lights blinking softly in the dusk. The friends worked together to gently catch them, being careful to keep the fireflies safe and happy. They placed them inside a small pouch made from soft leaves, creating a temporary home for the glowing creatures until the lantern was ready.

As they returned to the leaf pile, the sky was bathed in shades of pink, orange, and purple. The evening air was cool, and the friends felt a quiet excitement as they placed the fireflies into the Leaf Lantern, closing it carefully to keep the tiny lights safe inside.

When the first firefly blinked inside the lantern, a soft, golden glow spread through the leaves, illuminating the lantern with a warm, comforting light. More fireflies joined in, their little lights twinkling, filling the lantern with a gentle, magical glow. The friends sat around it, their faces illuminated by the soft light, each one feeling a sense of wonder and peace.

"Oh, it's perfect," whispered Willow, her eyes wide with awe.

Hazel leaned closer, her face glowing in the lantern's light. "It feels like a piece of the stars came down to join us."

The friends sat in silence, each one lost in the beauty of the moment. The lantern's warm light wrapped around them, making them feel safe, connected, and deeply grateful for the friendship they shared.

As they watched the fireflies blink and glow, Ember felt a surge of gratitude. The Leaf Lantern wasn't just a decoration—it was a symbol of the love, creativity, and teamwork that had brought it to life. It reminded him of the special bond he shared with his friends, and the joy they had found in creating something together.

After a while, Bramble spoke up, his voice soft with emotion. "This lantern feels like a part of all of us. We each added something special, and together, we made something beautiful."

The friends nodded, each one feeling the truth of his words. They had taken pieces of themselves—their ideas, their creativity, and their care—and woven them into something that brought light and warmth to their gathering place.

Ember smiled, his heart full. "I'm so glad we made this together. This lantern will always remind us of our friendship and the joy we find in each other's company."

As the stars began to appear in the sky, the friends snuggled closer, basking in the soft glow of their Leaf Lantern. They shared stories and laughter, each one feeling a deep sense of peace and contentment.

Eventually, as the fireflies' lights began to dim, they opened the lantern, letting the little creatures fly free into the night. The fireflies drifted away, their tiny lights blending with the stars above, and the friends watched them go with a sense of gratitude for the light they had shared.

When it was time to say goodbye, the friends hugged each other, their hearts filled with the warmth of the evening's memories. They knew that the Leaf Lantern would always hold a special place in their hearts, a symbol of the creativity, teamwork, and love they shared.

Chapter 15: The Stormy Surprise

The morning was calm and quiet in the Valley of Echoes, but a thick layer of gray clouds hung over the trees, casting a soft, shadowed light across the valley. Ember woke to the gentle rumble of thunder in the distance, a sound that made the leaves tremble and the air feel charged. A storm was coming, and Ember felt a sense of excitement mixed with concern as he thought of the leaf pile and the Leaf Lantern they had so carefully created.

As he reached the clearing, he saw that his friends were already gathered around the leaf pile, their faces filled with worry as they looked up at the sky. Bramble, Hazel, Clover, Midge, Nettle, Pip, and Willow huddled close together, whispering about the storm clouds and glancing toward the Leaf Lantern.

"Good morning, everyone!" Ember called, trying to keep his voice cheerful despite the darkening sky.

"Good morning, Ember!" his friends replied, their voices tinged with worry.

Ember joined them, looking at their beautiful Leaf Lantern, which sat in the middle of the leaf pile. It looked peaceful and inviting, filled with the memories of the warmth and joy they'd shared the previous evening. The thought of the storm damaging their creation filled Ember with a pang of sadness.

Hazel looked at him, her eyes wide with concern. "Do you think the storm will ruin our lantern, Ember?"

Ember took a deep breath, thinking carefully. "The storm might be strong, and it could scatter some of the leaves, but maybe we can work together to protect it."

The friends nodded, each one determined to do what they could to shield their creation. They had all poured their hearts into the Leaf Lantern, and they weren't ready to let it go so easily.

"We could try reinforcing it with stronger branches," Bramble suggested, always quick to think of practical solutions. "If we add a few thicker sticks to the base, it might withstand the wind better."

The friends agreed, and they immediately set to work, gathering sturdy sticks and vines from nearby trees. Ember and Bramble used the sticks to strengthen the frame, while Hazel and Pip carefully wrapped the vines around the lantern's structure, pulling them tight to make it as secure as possible.

Willow added a layer of leaves along the bottom, hoping the extra weight would help hold the lantern in place. Meanwhile, Midge and Nettle brought over small rocks to line the edges of the leaf pile, creating a ring that would help protect the lantern from the wind.

As they worked, the wind began to pick up, rustling the leaves and sending small gusts through the valley. The friends felt the chill in the air and hurried to complete their preparations, each one pouring their love and care into the work.

Once they had finished reinforcing the lantern, Ember stepped back, feeling a sense of pride as he looked at their creation. "We did everything we could," he said, his voice filled with hope. "Now we just have to wait and see."

The friends gathered around the lantern, huddling close as the wind grew stronger. They could feel the storm approaching, its presence like a quiet but powerful force that filled the valley with a charged stillness.

As the first raindrops began to fall, they felt a mixture of anticipation and worry. The rain was gentle at first, but soon it grew heavier, each drop pattering against the leaves and creating small rivulets that ran through the clearing. The friends stayed close, watching as the rain soaked the leaves, making the colors darker and more vibrant.

A gust of wind swept through the clearing, and the Leaf Lantern shuddered, its structure holding but swaying slightly under the force of the storm. Ember and his friends held their breath, hoping that their reinforcements would be enough.

But as the storm grew stronger, the wind howled through the valley, tugging at the leaves and sticks with increasing force. Another gust ripped through the clearing, and with a sudden, heart-wrenching creak, the Leaf Lantern tipped to one side. The friends gasped as they watched some of the leaves scatter, carried away by the wind.

"Oh no!" Clover cried, her voice filled with sadness. "Our lantern..."

Ember felt his heart sink as he watched their beloved lantern begin to unravel. Despite their best efforts, the storm was proving too strong, scattering the leaves and shaking the structure they had worked so hard to protect.

"Maybe we should step back," Willow suggested gently, her voice soft with understanding. "We've done everything we could, but sometimes we have to let things go and hope for the best."

The friends nodded reluctantly, each of them feeling the weight of the storm's power. They stepped back from the leaf pile, huddling together for warmth as they watched the storm take its course.

As they waited, the wind grew louder, and rain poured down, washing over the valley and soaking everything in sight. Ember felt a mix of sadness and acceptance as he watched the leaves scatter, knowing that the storm was beyond their control. But he also felt a deep sense of gratitude for the memories they had made together, for the joy and love that had gone into creating the Leaf Lantern.

When the storm finally began to calm, the rain eased to a gentle drizzle, and the wind softened, leaving the valley in a quiet, damp stillness. The friends looked at each other, each one feeling a sense of loss but also a quiet resilience.

Ember took a deep breath, turning to face the leaf pile. The lantern was mostly intact, but its walls were torn, and many of the leaves and decorations had been scattered by the wind. It no longer glowed with the magic it had held the previous night, but Ember felt a flicker of determination.

"We may have lost some of our lantern, but we can rebuild it," he said, his voice steady. "Just like before, we can create something beautiful together. The storm may have taken some of our work, but it didn't take away the joy we shared or the memories we made."

The friends accepted, each one feeling a renewed sense of purpose. They began gathering leaves, twigs, and acorns once more, determined to bring the lantern back to life. This time, their work felt different—there was a strength and resilience in their movements, a quiet understanding that beauty could be rebuilt even after it was lost.

Chapter 16: The Hidden Hollow

The next morning, the Valley of Echoes was bright and fresh, the ground sparkling with dew left behind by the previous night's storm. Ember awoke with a renewed sense of excitement, eager to see his friends and discover what the day had in store. After all they had been through together—building the Leaf Lantern, facing the storm, and rebuilding it—Ember felt ready for a new adventure.

As he reached the clearing, he found his friends waiting for him. Bramble, Hazel, Clover, Midge, Nettle, Pip, and Willow were gathered around the leaf pile, their faces bright with anticipation.

"Good morning, everyone!" Ember called, waving his paw.

"Good morning, Ember!" they replied in unison, their voices filled with cheer.

Ember noticed a new energy in the group. They all seemed eager and full of ideas, as if the storm had left them with a desire to explore the valley and discover more of the magic it held.

Hazel, ever the adventurous spirit, looked around at her friends with a mischievous grin. "I was thinking," she began, "we've played near the leaf pile for days, and we know this part of the valley by heart. What if we went exploring today to see if we can find new places we haven't discovered yet?"

The friends exchanged excited glances, each of them thrilled by the idea. The valley was vast and full of wonders, many of which they had never seen. The idea of exploring together filled them with a sense of curiosity and excitement.

"That sounds like a wonderful idea," Bramble agreed, his eyes twinkling. "There must be so many hidden spots we haven't seen yet."

Clover nodded eagerly. "I'd love to find a new place where we can play and make new memories. And maybe we'll find some special leaves or treasures to add to our leaf pile!"

The group cheered, and without further hesitation, they set off together, following Hazel's lead as they made their way beyond the familiar clearing and deeper into the valley.

They passed through a grove of tall oaks, their branches arching high overhead, creating a natural canopy that dappled the ground with patches of sunlight. Midge flew above them, her sharp eyes scanning the area for anything unusual or interesting.

After a short walk, they came across a small stream that babbled quietly as it wound its way through the forest. The water was clear and cool, and tiny fish darted between the rocks, their scales glinting in the sunlight.

"Look at those fish!" Pip exclaimed, his eyes wide with wonder. "They're so small and quick!"

The friends paused to watch the fish, their hearts filled with appreciation for the beauty of the valley. Each discovery, no matter how small, added a new layer of magic to their journey.

As they continued, the landscape began to change. The trees grew closer together, their branches twisting and weaving into each other. The ground was covered in a thick carpet of moss that felt soft and springy beneath their paws.

Willow stopped suddenly, her sharp eyes catching something unusual. "Look!" she whispered, pointing to a spot hidden between two large rocks. "There's a little opening over there. It looks like it leads to something."

Curiosity bubbled up in the group as they approached the rocks. Nestled between them was a small entrance, partly hidden by a curtain of ivy. The friends peered inside, their eyes adjusting to the dim light.

"It's a hollow!" Hazel exclaimed, her voice filled with excitement. "A hidden hollow!"

The friends exchanged excited glances, each one thrilled by the discovery. This hidden hollow, tucked away and unknown to them until now, felt like a secret treasure waiting to be explored.

With Ember leading the way, they carefully climbed through the ivy-covered entrance and into the hollow. Inside, they found a small, cozy space bathed in soft light filtering through gaps in the branches overhead. The walls of the hollow were covered in vines, and colorful mushrooms grew in clusters along the edges, their caps shimmering with dew.

"This place is amazing!" Clover whispered, her eyes wide with awe. "It feels like a little secret hideaway just for us."

Ember felt a surge of happiness as he looked around. The hollow was quiet and peaceful, a perfect spot for them to rest, play, and share stories. It felt like a new part of the valley that belonged to them alone.

They settled into the hollow, each friend finding a comfortable spot among the soft moss and leaves. As they sat together, the gentle light and the cozy surroundings filled them with a sense of calm and togetherness.

Hazel, who had brought along a small satchel of berries, passed them around. "This can be our adventure snack," she said with a grin. "Nothing like a sweet treat to celebrate our discovery!"

The friends laughed and thanked Hazel, savoring the juicy berries as they enjoyed the moment. Each bite felt like a celebration of their journey, a reminder of the bond they shared and the joy of exploring together.

As they finished their berries, Midge had an idea. "Since we found this hollow together, why don't we make it our secret meeting place?" she suggested. "We could come here whenever we want to share stories, play, or just be together."

The friends agreed, thrilled by the idea of having a hidden spot just for them. The hollow would be their special place, a sanctuary where they could gather, talk, and make memories.

Ember felt a sense of pride as he looked around at his friends. "Let's each add something to the hollow, something that represents us. That way, this place will truly feel like it belongs to all of us."

The friends nodded, each of them eager to leave their mark on the hollow. They spread out, searching for items that would make the space uniquely theirs.

Bramble found a small, smooth stone that fit perfectly in his paw. He placed it at the center of the hollow, marking it as a symbol of strength and stability. "This stone will remind us that our friendship is strong and steady," he said with a smile.

Clover brought a delicate fern leaf and tucked it into a crevice in the wall. "The fern will remind us to grow together, just like it grows in the forest."

Hazel added a pine cone she had found, its scales open and fragrant. "This pine cone will remind us of our adventures and the fun we have together."

Willow found a tiny feather and placed it near the entrance. "The feather will remind us to be gentle and kind with each other, like the soft touch of feathers."

Nettle found a small piece of bark shaped like a heart and set it near the wall of the hollow. "This heart-shaped bark will remind us of the love and care we share."

Pip brought over a pebble he had collected from the stream, its surface smooth and cool. "This pebble is from the stream we crossed. It'll remind us of the journey we took to find this place."

Midge fluttered over with a tiny, sparkling dewdrop leaf and set it near the center. "This dewdrop leaf will remind us to always look for beauty, even in small things."

Finally, Ember added a small cluster of red and orange leaves he had found along the way. He placed them near the stone, their colors vibrant against the moss. "These leaves will remind us of the warmth and joy of our friendship," he said, his voice full of gratitude.

As they looked around, each friend felt a sense of pride and connection. The hollow, once a simple hidden spot in the valley, was now filled with pieces of themselves, each item a symbol of their friendship and the journey they had taken together.

They spent the rest of the afternoon sharing stories, playing games, and laughing in their newfound sanctuary. The hollow became filled with the sound of their voices, a place that felt truly alive with friendship and love.

Chapter 17: A Visitor from Afar

The next morning, the Valley of Echoes was filled with the cheerful sounds of birdsong and the soft rustling of leaves. Ember made his way to the leaf pile, eager to see his friends and share the day with them. After discovering the hidden hollow the day before, Ember felt a renewed sense of adventure. He wondered what other surprises the valley might have in store for them.

As he reached the clearing, he found his friends already gathered around the leaf pile, chatting happily about their plans for the day. Bramble, Hazel, Clover, Midge, Nettle, Pip, and Willow greeted him with warm smiles, each of them full of excitement after their adventure.

"Good morning, everyone!" Ember called out, joining them with a bright smile.

"Good morning, Ember!" his friends replied, their faces lighting up.

As they settled into the leaf pile, sharing stories and laughter, they heard a soft rustling sound from the edge of the clearing. The friends looked up, curious, and saw a small, unfamiliar figure standing just beyond the trees. It was a young squirrel with bushy fur in shades of chestnut and gray, her eyes wide with wonder as she gazed at the leaf pile.

The squirrel hesitated, glancing around nervously. She looked shy and uncertain, as if she wasn't sure whether she was welcome. Ember felt a gentle warmth in his heart; he remembered the times he had felt nervous around new friends, and he wanted to make her feel as welcome as possible.

With a kind smile, he waved his paw, inviting her to come closer. "Hello there!" Ember called, his voice warm and friendly. "Would you like to join us?"

The squirrel's face brightened at his invitation, and she took a few hesitant steps forward. "Oh… thank you," she said softly, her voice barely a whisper. "My name is Tansy. I'm new to this part of the valley, and I wasn't sure if I would find any friendly faces here."

Hazel beamed, her tail flicking with excitement. "It's so nice to meet you, Tansy! We'd love to have you join us. We were just about to play some games together."

The friends introduced themselves, each one offering Tansy a warm welcome. She looked around at the friendly faces, her initial nervousness melting away as she felt the kindness in each of their smiles. It wasn't long before Tansy settled into the leaf pile beside them, her eyes filled with wonder at the cozy, colorful nest they had created.

"You have such a beautiful leaf pile," Tansy said, looking around with admiration. "It looks like a place full of fun and friendship."

Ember nodded, feeling a sense of pride. "This leaf pile has become a special place for all of us. We gather here every day to play, share stories, and enjoy each other's company."

Tansy's face softened, and she looked at them with gratitude. "I feel so lucky to have found you all. I've been traveling for days, hoping to find a place where I could feel at home. This... this feels like that place."

The friends exchanged smiles, each of them touched by Tansy's words. They wanted to make her feel as welcome as possible, knowing that the valley could be a warm and inviting home for her too.

Hazel, who always loved planning activities, clapped her paws together. "Let's play 'Leaf Toss'!" she suggested with a grin. "It's one of our favorite games. We each take turns tossing a leaf as high as we can, and the goal is to see who can catch it before it touches the ground!"

The friends cheered, excited to play their beloved game and eager to show Tansy how much fun they could have together. They each selected a bright, crinkly leaf, then lined up in a row, ready to take turns tossing their leaves into the air.

Ember went first, tossing his leaf with a gentle flick of his paw. It soared up, twisting and turning before he caught it just before it touched the ground. The friends cheered, and Tansy's eyes sparkled as she watched the game, clearly eager to try it herself.

When it was her turn, Tansy took a deep breath, carefully tossed her leaf into the air, and watched as it floated down. She reached out, catching it with a delighted giggle. The friends clapped and cheered, making her feel proud and included.

"You did great, Tansy!" Clover said, giving her an encouraging smile. "You're a natural at Leaf Toss!"

Tansy blushed with happiness, her confidence growing with each kind word. She felt more at ease than she had in days, grateful to have found friends who welcomed her so openly.

As they continued playing, Midge noticed that Tansy's face was still tinged with a hint of exhaustion. She fluttered over, her voice soft with concern. "Have you been traveling for a long time, Tansy?"

Tansy nodded, her smile fading slightly. "Yes, I've been looking for a new home. My family had to move from our old tree, and I got separated from them in the journey. I hoped I'd find them here, but… it's been difficult."

Ember's heart ached for Tansy, and he felt a deep desire to help her feel comforted. "You're welcome to stay here with us, Tansy," he said gently. "And if you need help finding your family, we can all look for them together."

The friends nodded, each of them filled with a sense of purpose. They wanted Tansy to know she wasn't alone and that they would be there to support her.

Tansy's eyes filled with gratitude, and she took a deep breath, her voice soft but steady. "Thank you, everyone. I'd love to stay here with you. You've made me feel like I've found a place where I belong."

The friends gathered around her, their hearts full of warmth. They knew that the valley could be a place of comfort and joy for Tansy, just as it had been for each of them.

To celebrate her arrival, Ember suggested they each share one of their favorite games or activities with Tansy. "Let's show Tansy all the fun things we love to do here," he said, smiling at his friends.

Hazel began by teaching her how to play "Leaf Hop," a game where they each had to hop from one leaf to another without touching the ground. Tansy laughed as she joined in, her eyes gleaming with excitement as she tried to balance on the leaves.

Next, Bramble showed her "Twig Balance," a game where they each placed a twig on their nose and tried to keep it balanced as they walked. Tansy wobbled at first, but with Bramble's guidance, she soon found her footing, giggling as she managed to keep the twig steady.

Willow, who had a gentle and calming nature, suggested they try "Pebble Count," a quiet game where they each counted pebbles around the leaf pile, seeing who could find the most. Tansy enjoyed the peaceful challenge, and the friends shared gentle laughter as they admired each other's collections.

As the sun dipped lower in the sky, Ember noticed that Tansy's face was filled with joy, her earlier sadness and exhaustion replaced by a look of peace and happiness. She had found not just a place to rest, but a circle of friends who had welcomed her with open hearts.

Before they ended their day, Clover reached into her satchel and pulled out a small, colorful scarf she had woven from soft strands of grass and delicate flower petals. She held it out to Tansy with a warm smile.

"This is for you, Tansy," Clover said gently. "It's something I made with love, and I'd like you to have it as a reminder that you're always welcome here."

Tansy's eyes shimmered with gratitude as she took the scarf, wrapping it around her neck. "Thank you, Clover. This is the kindest gift I've ever received. I'll wear it every day to remind myself of the friends I've found here."

The friends gathered around her, each of them feeling the warmth of their connection. Tansy had brought a new joy to their group, and they felt grateful for the chance to welcome her, knowing that their valley had grown a little brighter with her presence.

Chapter 18: The Festival of Friendship

The morning sun rose over the Valley of Echoes, casting a warm glow across the treetops as Ember made his way to the leaf pile. He felt an extra burst of excitement today, inspired by the kindness his friends had shown to Tansy the day before. Ember wanted to celebrate the joy and love they had found together, and he had an idea that would make the day one they'd never forget.

As he reached the clearing, he saw his friends gathered, chatting and laughing, their faces bright with the happiness that had filled their hearts since welcoming Tansy into their group. Bramble, Hazel, Clover, Midge, Nettle, Pip, Willow, and Tansy all looked up as he arrived, each one giving him a warm smile.

"Good morning, everyone!" Ember greeted, waving his paw.

"Good morning, Ember!" his friends replied, their voices filled with cheer.

Ember settled into the leaf pile with them, his eyes twinkling with excitement. "I had an idea last night," he began. "I thought we could create our very own celebration—a Festival of Friendship!"

The friends exchanged delighted glances, intrigued by the idea.

"A festival?" Tansy asked, her voice soft with wonder. "What would we do?"

"Well," Ember explained, "we could decorate the clearing with leaves, flowers, and twinkling lights from the fireflies. Each of us can share something special with the group, like a story, a song, or a game. We'll celebrate everything that makes our friendships unique and give thanks for each other."

The friends cheered, each one thrilled by the thought of creating their own festival. It would be a day filled with joy, laughter, and gratitude, a chance to express how much they meant to one another.

Hazel clapped her paws together, her tail swishing with excitement. "Let's start with decorations! We could gather colorful leaves, wildflowers, and maybe even some shiny pebbles from the riverbank."

The friends nodded in agreement, and they immediately set off to gather materials, their hearts full of excitement for the celebration to come.

Ember, Bramble, and Willow headed toward the riverbank, where they found smooth, glistening pebbles in shades of gray, white, and deep green. Each pebble caught the light in a different way, and they carefully selected the ones that sparkled the most.

Meanwhile, Hazel, Clover, and Midge gathered flowers from a nearby meadow, selecting bright red poppies, golden marigolds, and delicate blue forget-me-nots. The flowers added a beautiful array of colors, and the friends were careful to pick only a few from each patch, leaving plenty behind for the bees and butterflies.

Tansy and Pip found vibrant leaves in shades of orange, yellow, and red, each one as crisp and beautiful as the last. They also gathered a few sprigs of fragrant herbs, adding a fresh scent to the decorations.

As they returned to the clearing, the friends worked together to arrange their treasures around the leaf pile, creating a festive, colorful space that radiated warmth and joy. They scattered the pebbles in a circle, creating a sparkling border, and draped the flowers and leaves around the edges of the pile, weaving them into garlands that hung gracefully from the branches.

When the decorations were complete, they all stepped back, admiring their handiwork.

"It's beautiful," whispered Willow, her eyes shining with happiness. "This feels like a place made just for us."

Ember nodded, his heart full of pride. "We made this together, and that's what makes it so special. Now, let's start our Festival of Friendship!"

The friends gathered in a circle around the leaf pile, each one eager to share something meaningful with the group. Ember went first, his voice warm and full of gratitude.

"I want to thank each of you," he said softly. "This valley has become a home for me because of the love and kindness we share. I'm grateful for the way we lift each other up, through every adventure and challenge. Today, I want to celebrate the joy of having friends like you."

The group murmured in appreciation, each of them touched by Ember's words. They felt the same gratitude for him, knowing that his warmth and care had brought them all closer together.

Next, Clover stood up, her eyes shining with excitement. "I'd like to share a game called 'Petal Dance!'" she announced. "Each of us will take a flower petal, and we'll see how long we can keep it in the air by blowing on it. The goal is to make the petals float together, like a dance!"

The friends cheered, eager to try the new game. They each selected a colorful petal and gathered in a circle, holding their petals up to the breeze. On the count of three, they let go, gently blowing to keep their petals afloat.

Laughter filled the air as they watched the petals drift and twirl, moving together in a delicate, colorful dance. They took turns blowing on the petals, their laughter ringing through the valley as they tried to keep the petals floating as long as possible.

After several rounds, they settled back into the leaf pile, still giggling from the fun. Tansy, who had been watching with wide eyes, stood up next.

"I... I'd like to share something too," she said shyly. "It's a song my family used to sing when we gathered together. It always made me feel loved, and I'd like to share that feeling with all of you."

The friends nodded, their faces warm with encouragement, and Tansy took a deep breath, closing her eyes as she began to sing.

Her voice was soft and sweet, filling the clearing with a melody that was gentle and full of love. The words spoke of friendship, of the warmth and safety found in each other's company, and of the joy that came from sharing life's journey together. As she sang, the friends listened with quiet reverence, each of them feeling a deep connection to Tansy's song.

When she finished, they all clapped, their eyes bright with emotion.

"That was beautiful, Tansy," Midge said, her voice full of admiration. "Thank you for sharing that with us."

Tansy smiled, her heart full of gratitude. She felt deeply connected to her friends, knowing that her song had brought them closer.

Later, Midge suggested they gather some fireflies to light up the clearing. The friends agreed, and they gently collected a few fireflies, placing them around the leaf pile. Their tiny lights began to twinkle, creating a magical glow that filled the clearing with warmth.

With the fireflies lighting up the night, the friends took turns sharing stories, games, and heartfelt words of appreciation. Each friend brought something unique, and together they created a celebration filled with laughter, love, and gratitude.

Chapter 19: The Story of the Valley

The sun rose gently over the Valley of Echoes, casting a warm glow across the landscape and filling the air with the cheerful sounds of birdsong. Ember made his way to the leaf pile, feeling a deep sense of contentment after the Festival of Friendship they'd shared the night before. He thought of the laughter, games, and gratitude that had filled the clearing, grateful for the love that bound him to his friends.

As he arrived, he found Bramble, Hazel, Clover, Midge, Nettle, Pip, Willow, and Tansy already gathered around, chatting softly as they enjoyed the morning's quiet peace. Ember settled beside them, savoring the calm, but he sensed a shared curiosity lingering in the air.

"Good morning, everyone!" Ember greeted, smiling warmly at his friends.

"Good morning, Ember!" they chorused, their faces lighting up as he joined them.

They chatted for a while, sharing memories of the festival and reflecting on their favorite moments. But Ember noticed that his friends kept glancing around the valley, as if searching for something hidden among the trees. He followed their gaze, wondering what had captured their attention.

Hazel spoke up, breaking the silence. "Have you ever wondered about the history of this valley?" she asked, her voice filled with curiosity. "I mean, we all found this place, and it's become our home, but who else might have called it home before us?"

The question seemed to spark a quiet wonder among the group. They'd shared so many special moments in the valley, but they hadn't thought much about its past. Ember felt his heart quicken with curiosity—he wanted to know the stories that lay hidden in the valley's trees, rivers, and rocks.

LEO AND THE LEAF PILE

Just as they were deep in thought, they heard the soft, wise voice of someone approaching. "I can tell you about the history of the Valley of Echoes, if you'd like," the voice said.

The friends turned to see an old owl perched on a low branch nearby. Her feathers were soft and silvery, touched with hints of brown and gray, and her large eyes glowed with kindness and wisdom. It was Olwen, the wise elder of the valley, known for her vast knowledge and gentle spirit.

"Good morning, Olwen!" Ember greeted her respectfully, his heart filled with admiration. "We'd love to hear the stories of the valley. We've all been so curious about who might have lived here before us."

Olwen nodded, her eyes twinkling with warmth. "The valley holds many stories, my friends," she said softly. "It has been a home to creatures of all kinds, each leaving a piece of themselves behind, like leaves that fall and become part of the forest floor."

The friends gathered closer, their faces bright with anticipation as Olwen began to speak.

"Long, long ago," Olwen began, "the valley was home to a family of foxes who called themselves the MeadowClan. They were strong, wise, and kind, and they respected the land deeply, treating it with care and gratitude. They lived in harmony with the trees, rivers, and plants, believing that every part of the valley held a spirit to be honored."

Clover's eyes widened with wonder. "The MeadowClan sounds amazing. Did they do anything special to take care of the valley?"

Olwen nodded, her eyes gleaming with pride for the ancient foxes. "Indeed they did, Clover. The MeadowClan would hold gatherings each season, much like your Festival of Friendship, to give thanks for the valley's beauty and abundance. They would share stories of their ancestors, dance beneath the stars, and leave gifts of flowers and herbs by the riverbank as offerings to the spirits of the valley."

The friends listened in awe, each of them picturing the MeadowClan celebrating under the same stars they had danced beneath the night before. It was a humbling thought, and they felt a newfound respect for the valley and those who had lived there long ago.

"After the MeadowClan moved on," Olwen continued, "a family of deer called the MistFolk came to live in the valley. They were gentle and graceful, known for their ability to move silently through the forest. The MistFolk believed that every creature in the valley had a purpose, and they practiced kindness and patience with all living things."

Pip leaned forward, his eyes wide with fascination. "What kinds of things did the MistFolk do to show their kindness, Olwen?"

Olwen smiled, her voice soft with admiration. "The MistFolk were known for caring for the sick and injured creatures of the valley. They would offer food and shelter to anyone in need, even if they were different from themselves. They believed that every creature deserved compassion, and they taught this lesson to all who came after them."

The friends were quiet for a moment, each of them feeling a deep sense of respect for the MistFolk's kindness. The valley was more than just a place to play and share laughter—it was a sanctuary of love, where kindness had been woven into its very heart.

"After the MistFolk left," Olwen continued, "a group of birds called the SkySeekers found their home here. They were explorers, filled with curiosity and a desire to see every corner of the valley. The SkySeekers believed that the valley was a place of discovery, a gift meant to be explored and appreciated."

Hazel's face lit up with excitement. "They sound like adventurers! Did they find any special places in the valley?"

"Oh, they certainly did," Olwen said with a nod. "The SkySeekers mapped every tree, river, and hill, giving each place a name and sharing their findings with others. They left markings in the trees, stones by the river, and small feathers near hidden clearings, creating a trail of clues for anyone who wished to follow in their footsteps."

The friends exchanged excited glances, each one eager to explore the valley for signs left by the SkySeekers. Knowing that explorers had wandered these same paths, leaving behind traces of their adventures, made the valley feel even more magical.

"Finally," Olwen continued, her voice growing soft, "the valley welcomed the Wanderers, a group of animals of all shapes and sizes who had come from many different places. They had been searching for a home, a place where they could be free to live in harmony, and they found that here in the Valley of Echoes. The Wanderers brought new traditions, each one adding their own spirit to the valley."

Willow's eyes filled with warmth. "So the valley has always been a place of friendship and kindness?"

Olwen nodded, her eyes twinkling. "Yes, Willow. The valley is a place where all creatures can come together, bringing their unique gifts and leaving behind memories of love and unity. Every creature who has lived here has added to its beauty and magic, just as each of you has."

Ember felt his heart swell with pride and gratitude. The valley wasn't just a beautiful place—it was a tapestry of stories, woven together by generations of creatures who had loved, cared for, and respected the land.

"Thank you for sharing these stories, Olwen," Ember said, his voice full of respect. "We'll do our best to honor the valley and continue its traditions."

The friends murmured in agreement, each of them feeling a renewed sense of responsibility for the valley they called home. They wanted to carry on the legacy of kindness, respect, and gratitude that had been left by those who came before.

Olwen smiled, her eyes filled with pride. "I know you will, my friends. The valley's history lives on through each of you, and as long as you continue to love and care for this place, its spirit will remain strong."

Olwen bid them farewell, her wings gliding gracefully as she disappeared into the trees. The friends watched her go, their hearts full of gratitude for the wisdom she had shared.

They spent the rest of the afternoon walking through the valley, their eyes wide with wonder as they noticed each tree, rock, and river in a new light. Every part of the valley felt alive with history, and they felt a deep connection to the creatures who had lived there before them.

Before they returned to the leaf pile, Ember suggested they each make a small offering to the valley in honor of its past. They gathered wildflowers, pebbles, and leaves, placing them by the riverbank as a symbol of their respect and gratitude.

Chapter 20: The Mysterious Marks

The next morning in the Valley of Echoes was bright and clear, with the sunlight filtering through the trees and casting soft, golden patches across the forest floor. After learning about the valley's history from Olwen the day before, Ember and his friends felt a new sense of wonder for the place they called home. Each path, tree, and river seemed to carry a story, and they wanted to uncover as much of it as possible.

As he reached the leaf pile, Ember saw his friends already gathered, their eyes sparkling with excitement. Bramble, Hazel, Clover, Midge, Nettle, Pip, Willow, and Tansy greeted him eagerly, each one clearly still enchanted by the tales of the MeadowClan, the MistFolk, the SkySeekers, and the Wanderers.

"Good morning, everyone!" Ember greeted, waving a paw.

"Good morning, Ember!" they replied, their voices filled with cheer.

Hazel, who had a natural curiosity, was the first to speak up. "I was thinking," she began, her voice full of energy, "since Olwen told us about the SkySeekers leaving marks around the valley, maybe we could search for them today! Who knows what we might find?"

The friends exchanged excited glances, thrilled by the idea of going on a mystery hunt through the valley. The thought of finding marks or clues left by the SkySeekers—the brave explorers who had mapped the valley long ago—filled them with a sense of adventure.

Ember nodded, feeling his own excitement build. "That sounds like a wonderful idea, Hazel. Let's see what mysteries we can uncover!"

With that, the group set off, each friend brimming with anticipation. They decided to start near the stream, where they had often found smooth pebbles and tiny flowers. It seemed like the kind of place where explorers might have left signs for others to follow.

As they walked along the stream, their eyes carefully scanned the ground, trees, and rocks for any unusual markings or hidden symbols.

Bramble, always the observant one, noticed a faint scratch on the bark of a tree. It was a simple arrow shape, pointing toward a cluster of bushes nearby.

"Look here!" Bramble called, his eyes gleaming with excitement. "I think this might be one of the SkySeekers' marks!"

The friends gathered around, studying the arrow with fascination. It was faint and weathered, but its shape was clear enough for them to recognize. Their hearts quickened with excitement—this was the first clue in their journey!

"Let's follow it," Midge suggested, her wings fluttering with excitement. "Maybe it leads to something special."

They followed the arrow's direction, pushing gently through the bushes until they reached a small clearing. In the center was a large, flat stone, its surface etched with more markings. The friends knelt down, their eyes wide as they examined the stone.

On the stone were small circles, triangles, and lines that seemed to form a pattern. It looked like a map, with the lines representing pathways, and the triangles marking significant spots.

"This must be one of the SkySeekers' maps!" Tansy whispered, her voice filled with wonder. "They left it here to show others the way."

The friends studied the map closely, each of them trying to understand its meaning. It seemed to show a series of paths winding through the valley, with certain points marked by triangles. One of the triangles was right near the river, just like where they were standing.

Hazel traced a path on the stone with her paw. "I think this is where we are," she said, her voice thoughtful. "And if we follow this line here, it looks like there's another spot marked farther into the valley."

Ember's heart raced with excitement. "Let's see where it leads! The SkySeekers must have left something special for explorers like us to find."

With the stone map as their guide, the friends continued their journey, their eyes scanning the valley for any further signs or markings.

They felt like true explorers, each step filled with anticipation and curiosity.

As they followed the map's path, they came across another mark—a circle carved into a tree stump, with an arrow pointing toward a small hill in the distance. The friends felt a thrill as they continued onward, knowing they were walking in the footsteps of the SkySeekers.

After a while, they reached the hill marked on the map, and at its base, they discovered a small, hollowed-out nook in the ground. Inside the nook was an old, weathered feather, nestled carefully between two stones. It was long and gray, with small speckles along its edges—a feather that had once belonged to the SkySeekers themselves.

Midge gently picked up the feather, her eyes shining with wonder. "This must be a SkySeeker feather. They left it here as a gift for future explorers."

The friends gathered around, each of them touched by the idea of holding a piece of the valley's history. The feather felt like a symbol of all the SkySeekers' adventures, of the discoveries they had made and the love they'd felt for the valley.

"Let's bring it back to the leaf pile," Ember suggested. "We can place it there as a reminder of the SkySeekers and the journey they took through the valley."

The friends agreed, each one feeling a deep sense of respect for the SkySeekers' legacy. They carefully wrapped the feather in a soft leaf, treating it with the reverence it deserved, and began their journey back to the leaf pile.

As they walked, they talked about all they had discovered that day. The marks, the stone map, and the feather had given them a glimpse into the past, showing them how the SkySeekers had left pieces of their journey for others to follow.

When they reached the leaf pile, they placed the feather in a small alcove they created with leaves and pebbles. The feather sat at the center, surrounded by their own little treasures—a symbol of the connection between the past and the present.

Ember turned to his friends, his voice filled with gratitude. "Today was more than just an adventure. It was a reminder of the valley's history and of the explorers who loved this place as much as we do. I'm grateful that we could walk in their footsteps and learn from their journey."

The friends nodded, each of them feeling a quiet pride in being part of the valley's story. They knew that their own adventures would become a chapter in the valley's history, a part of the legacy they would one day leave for others to discover.

The friends rested in the leaf pile, watching the sky change from blue to shades of pink and orange. They felt a deep sense of peace, knowing they were connected to a larger story, a story that had begun long before them and would continue long after.

Willow, who had been quietly reflecting, spoke up. "I hope that one day, others will come here and discover the marks we've left behind. Maybe they'll wonder about us, just like we wondered about the SkySeekers."

Ember nodded, his heart full of hope. "We're part of the valley now, and it's part of us. Our friendships, our laughter, and our memories will be woven into this place, just like the SkySeekers' feather and the MeadowClan's gatherings."

They sat in comfortable silence, each one feeling a quiet reverence for the valley and the legacy they were creating together. The feather in the leaf pile was a symbol of that legacy, a reminder that they were part of something greater than themselves.

Chapter 21: The Memory Book

The morning sun rose softly over the Valley of Echoes, casting a warm light through the trees and filling the air with the sounds of chirping birds and rustling leaves. Ember arrived at the leaf pile with a new idea buzzing in his mind—a way to honor all the adventures he and his friends had shared. After their journey in search of the SkySeekers' marks, Ember felt inspired to capture their own memories, ensuring that their time together would be remembered for years to come.

As he reached the clearing, he found his friends already gathered around, chatting happily about their recent discoveries. Bramble, Hazel, Clover, Midge, Nettle, Pip, Willow, and Tansy greeted him with bright smiles, their faces glowing with the joy of friendship.

"Good morning, everyone!" Ember called out, joining them with a cheerful wave.

"Good morning, Ember!" they chorused, their voices filled with warmth.

Ember settled into the leaf pile, his eyes shining with excitement. "I had an idea last night," he began. "What if we made a Memory Book—a place where we can write down all our adventures, stories, and special moments together?"

The friends exchanged curious glances, intrigued by the idea. The thought of creating a book to capture their memories filled them with excitement and wonder.

"A Memory Book?" Bramble repeated, his eyes lighting up. "That sounds amazing! We could write about all the fun games we've played and the places we've explored."

Hazel's tail swished with enthusiasm. "And we could add drawings, too! Pictures of our leaf pile, the hidden hollow, and even the marks we found left by the SkySeekers."

The friends nodded eagerly, each of them filled with ideas for the Memory Book. They wanted to create something that would capture the spirit of their friendship—a record of the laughter, kindness, and joy that had brought them together in the valley.

"We could also add little mementos," Clover suggested, her voice soft with excitement. "Maybe a colorful leaf or a small pebble from one of our adventures."

Tansy's eyes sparkled. "And songs! We could write down the songs we sing, so we never forget them."

Ember felt a warmth in his heart as he listened to his friends' ideas. The Memory Book would be more than just a collection of stories—it would be a celebration of the bond they shared, something they could look back on together, even as the years passed.

"Let's get started!" Midge chirped, her wings fluttering with excitement. "But... we'll need something sturdy to make the book."

The friends nodded, and they immediately set off to gather materials, each of them determined to find the perfect items to create their Memory Book. Bramble and Hazel went in search of large, sturdy leaves that would form the pages, while Clover and Pip looked for thin, flexible vines to bind the pages together.

Ember, Midge, and Willow headed toward the riverbank, searching for smooth stones and colorful pebbles that they could use to decorate the cover. The gentle murmur of the water filled the air, and as they sifted through the pebbles, they found stones in shades of red, green, and blue, each one polished smooth by the flowing water.

After gathering their materials, they returned to the leaf pile, where they began carefully assembling the Memory Book. Ember and Bramble worked together to layer the large leaves, creating a sturdy foundation. The leaves had a rich, earthy scent, and their varied shades of green and brown gave the book a natural beauty.

Hazel and Clover used the vines to bind the leaves along one edge, weaving them tightly to create a durable spine. The friends marveled at the way the vines held the leaves together, making their Memory Book feel strong and lasting.

Once the book was assembled, they placed the colorful pebbles on the cover, arranging them in a pattern that reflected the beauty of the valley. Midge added a delicate feather she had found, tucking it between the pebbles to give the cover an extra touch of magic.

When the book was complete, the friends stepped back to admire their work. The Memory Book was simple yet beautiful, filled with the love and care they had poured into each step of its creation.

"It's perfect," Willow whispered, her eyes shining with happiness. "I can already feel the memories waiting to be written inside."

Ember smiled, feeling a deep sense of pride. "Let's start by writing about our favorite memories so far. That way, we can capture the stories that mean the most to us."

The friends agreed, and they gathered around, each one eager to share their memories. Ember picked up a small stick to use as a pen, dipping it into a mixture of crushed berries that Clover had prepared, creating a natural ink.

With careful, deliberate strokes, Ember wrote the title on the first page: *The Memory Book of the Valley of Echoes.*

The friends cheered, their hearts full of excitement as Ember turned to the next page, ready to record their stories. They took turns sharing their memories, each friend adding something special to the book.

Hazel went first, her voice full of energy. "I want to write about the time we found the hidden hollow," she said. "It was such an amazing discovery, and we made it our secret meeting place."

Ember carefully wrote down Hazel's memory, capturing her words as she described the joy of finding the hollow and the wonder they had felt. He added a small drawing of the hollow, showing the vines, mushrooms, and soft moss that had made it feel like their own magical sanctuary.

Next, Bramble shared his memory of the Festival of Friendship. "That day meant so much to me," he said softly. "It was a celebration of our friendship, and it reminded me how lucky I am to have all of you."

Ember wrote down Bramble's words, adding a small sketch of the leaf pile decorated with flowers and pebbles. He carefully captured the warmth and joy of the festival, knowing it was a memory they would always cherish.

As each friend shared a memory, Ember added it to the book. They talked about their adventure in finding the SkySeekers' marks, their games of "Leaf Toss" and "Twig Balance," and the songs they had sung together. Each memory was filled with laughter and love, creating a beautiful tapestry of stories that reflected their journey.

When it was Tansy's turn, she took a deep breath, her voice soft with emotion. "I want to remember the day I met all of you," she said. "I had been searching for a place to belong, and finding this valley—and each of you—changed my life. I felt like I had found my family."

The friends nodded, touched by her words. Ember wrote down Tansy's memory, adding a drawing of her with the scarf Clover had given her, a symbol of the love and welcome she had received.

After each friend had shared a memory, they turned to the last page, leaving it blank. Ember placed a paw on the page, looking at his friends with a smile.

"This page is for the future," he said. "For all the adventures and memories we haven't made yet. It will remind us that our journey is still unfolding, and that we'll keep adding to this book as long as we're together."

The friends shook their heads, each one feeling a quiet excitement for the memories yet to come. The Memory Book was more than just a collection of stories—it was a promise, a way to capture the love, laughter, and friendship that filled their lives.

The friends sat together, gazing at their Memory Book. They felt a deep sense of peace, knowing that their memories were safe, written down for them to cherish and revisit whenever they wished.

Willow, who had been quietly reflecting, spoke up. "The Memory Book feels like a part of us," she said softly. "It's a reminder of everything we've shared and everything we will share."

Ember nodded, his heart full of gratitude. "We're part of the valley now, and this book will hold our story, just like the SkySeekers' feather and the MeadowClan's gatherings."

They closed the Memory Book carefully, tucking it safely among the leaves in their pile. It was a symbol of their journey, a legacy they could hold close, and a gift for future generations who might one day find it and wonder about the friends who had loved the Valley of Echoes.

Chapter 22: Preparing for the Harvest Gathering

As the morning sun cast a warm glow over the Valley of Echoes, Ember awoke with a feeling of excitement and purpose. Today, he and his friends had a special plan—to organize the valley's first-ever Harvest Gathering. The idea had come to him the night before, as he thought of the beautiful autumn leaves, the crisp air, and the bounty of nature that surrounded them. Ember wanted to celebrate the valley's gifts with his friends, creating a day filled with gratitude, joy, and togetherness.

As he arrived at the leaf pile, Ember saw his friends already gathered, their faces bright with anticipation. Bramble, Hazel, Clover, Midge, Nettle, Pip, Willow, and Tansy greeted him eagerly, their eyes sparkling with excitement as they waited to hear about the day's plans.

"Good morning, everyone!" Ember greeted, waving his paw warmly.

"Good morning, Ember!" they replied in unison, their voices filled with cheer.

Ember settled into the leaf pile with a smile, his heart brimming with enthusiasm. "I had an idea," he began. "What if we held a Harvest Gathering to celebrate everything the valley has given us? We can decorate the clearing, share our favorite foods, and play games together. It'll be a day to enjoy the beauty of autumn and give thanks for our friendship."

The friends exchanged delighted glances, thrilled by the idea. A Harvest Gathering sounded like the perfect way to honor the season and celebrate their bond.

"That sounds amazing, Ember!" Hazel said, her tail flicking with excitement. "I can already picture the decorations—bright autumn leaves, berries, and maybe even some wildflowers."

Bramble nodded, his face full of enthusiasm. "And we could each bring something special to share. I've been collecting acorns and chestnuts from the trees, and they'd make a perfect snack for everyone."

The friends began sharing ideas, each one eager to contribute to the Harvest Gathering. They wanted to create a day filled with warmth, laughter, and appreciation for the valley and each other.

"We'll need to plan everything carefully," Ember said, his voice thoughtful. "Let's divide the tasks so that everyone can help with something. That way, we'll make sure the gathering is perfect."

The friends agreed, and they quickly organized themselves, each one taking on a different task to bring the Harvest Gathering to life.

Hazel and Clover volunteered to gather decorations. They planned to collect colorful leaves, wildflowers, and berries to create a beautiful, festive space for the gathering. The thought of turning the clearing into a place of autumn beauty filled them with excitement.

Bramble and Nettle offered to gather food. They would collect acorns, chestnuts, and any other treats they could find, creating a bountiful feast for everyone to enjoy.

Midge and Willow decided to prepare games for the gathering. They wanted to plan activities that would be fun for everyone, creating a day filled with laughter and joy.

Ember and Tansy took on the role of organizing the event, making sure everything was in place and coordinating with each friend to bring their ideas together. Ember felt grateful for Tansy's help, knowing that her gentle spirit and attention to detail would make the day even more special.

With their tasks decided, the friends set off, each one eager to begin preparing for the Harvest Gathering. The valley buzzed with excitement as they worked, their hearts filled with the joy of creating something beautiful together.

Hazel and Clover wandered through the forest, their eyes scanning the ground for the most colorful leaves and wildflowers. They found bright red and orange maple leaves, golden birch leaves, and delicate blue forget-me-nots, gathering them carefully in bundles.

"We'll use the leaves to decorate the leaf pile," Hazel said, her eyes gleaming with excitement. "It'll look so festive and warm."

Clover smiled, holding up a small cluster of purple berries. "And these berries will add a lovely touch. We can hang them like little ornaments!"

The two friends returned to the clearing with their treasures, arranging the leaves, flowers, and berries around the leaf pile and throughout the clearing. The decorations filled the space with color and warmth, creating an inviting atmosphere that felt perfect for the Harvest Gathering.

Meanwhile, Bramble and Nettle were busy gathering food. They found acorns and chestnuts nestled at the bases of trees, their smooth, round shapes perfect for the feast. Nettle also discovered a few patches of wild mushrooms, carefully selecting the safe ones to add to their collection.

"These will make a delicious snack," Bramble said, his voice filled with pride. "We'll have a feast fit for everyone in the valley!"

Nettle smiled, arranging the food in a small pile. "I can't wait to share it with everyone. The valley has given us so much, and today feels like the perfect day to give thanks."

With the food gathered, they returned to the clearing, arranging their bounty in the center, ready to be enjoyed by all.

At the same time, Midge and Willow were busy planning games. They came up with several fun activities that would bring laughter and excitement to the gathering. One of their favorite ideas was a game called "Leaf Catch," where each friend would try to catch as many falling leaves as possible before they touched the ground.

"This will be so much fun!" Midge chirped, her wings fluttering with excitement. "We can all laugh and play together, and it'll be the perfect way to celebrate the season."

Willow nodded, her eyes filled with anticipation. "And I thought of a quiet game, too. We could play 'Guess the Sound,' where each friend makes a different nature sound, and we take turns guessing what it is."

The friends loved the idea, knowing it would add a special, peaceful touch to the day. With their games prepared, they joined the others in the clearing, ready to bring joy and laughter to the gathering.

As the sun reached its highest point, Ember and Tansy surveyed the preparations with pride. The clearing was beautifully decorated, the food was arranged in a lovely display, and the games were ready to go. Everything was in place for a perfect Harvest Gathering.

"Thank you, everyone," Ember said, his voice filled with gratitude. "This gathering wouldn't have been possible without each of you. Today, we celebrate not just the valley, but the friendship we share."

The friends gathered in a circle, feeling the warmth of their bond as they prepared to begin the Harvest Gathering. They started with a quiet moment of thanks, each friend reflecting on what they were grateful for—whether it was the beauty of the valley, the joy of friendship, or the simple pleasures of food and laughter.

After their moment of gratitude, they moved to the games. Leaf Catch was a huge success, with everyone laughing as they tried to catch as many falling leaves as they could. Ember and Hazel both managed to catch four leaves each, tying as the champions of the game.

Next, they played Guess the Sound. Each friend took turns making different nature sounds—the rustling of leaves, the chirping of birds, the soft bubbling of the river. The game brought moments of quiet joy, reminding them of the simple beauty in the valley's sounds.

After the games, they gathered around the food, sharing acorns, chestnuts, and mushrooms. Each bite was a reminder of the valley's abundance, a gift that they all felt grateful to share.

Ember looked around at his friends, his heart full. "Today has been a reminder of how lucky we are to have each other and this beautiful valley. I hope we can make the Harvest Gathering a tradition, something we celebrate every year."

The friends nodded, each of them feeling the same warmth and joy at the thought of making the Harvest Gathering a lasting tradition. The day had brought them closer, filling their hearts with gratitude for each other and the beauty of their home.

Tansy stood up, her eyes shining with an idea. "Since today is a celebration, I thought it would be nice to end with a circle of wishes. Each of us can make a wish for the valley, for our friendship, or for the future. Something special to carry forward."

The friends loved Tansy's idea and eagerly gathered in a circle, holding paws and wings, ready to share their wishes.

Ember started, his voice filled with warmth. "My wish is that our friendship remains as strong as it is today, no matter where life takes us. I hope we continue to laugh, support each other, and celebrate the valley's beauty together."

The friends smiled, feeling Ember's words resonate in their hearts. They felt the same deep connection and gratitude, knowing that their friendship was a gift they cherished.

Bramble was next, his voice steady and sincere. "My wish is for the valley to stay healthy and full of life, for all the plants, trees, and animals to flourish. This place has given us so much, and I hope it remains as beautiful as it is now, for us and for those who come after."

The friends nodded, their hearts touched by Bramble's love for the valley and its natural wonders.

Hazel, always full of energy and curiosity, shared her wish with a playful smile. "I wish for many more adventures together! May we always have new games to play, new places to explore, and new memories to make!"

The friends giggled, loving Hazel's wish. They knew that with each new day, the valley held countless surprises waiting for them.

Clover spoke softly, her voice filled with gentle kindness. "My wish is that each of us always feels at home here, surrounded by love and laughter. May we always find peace and comfort in each other's company."

The friends squeezed each other's paws, feeling the warmth of Clover's wish wrap around them like a cozy blanket.

Midge's wish was next, her wings fluttering as she spoke. "I wish that each of us continues to find beauty in small things—the sparkle of dew on a leaf, the song of a bird, or the sound of the river. May we never lose our wonder for the world around us."

The friends gazed at Midge with admiration, her love for life's simple joys filling their hearts with appreciation.

Willow, always gentle and thoughtful, shared her wish quietly. "My wish is for all of us to carry the kindness we share here with everyone we meet. May our friendship inspire us to spread love and compassion throughout the valley."

The friends nodded, each of them touched by Willow's wish. They knew that kindness was a gift they could always share with others.

Nettle's voice was soft but steady as she shared her wish. "I wish that we always remember this day and the joy we felt. Even when things change, may we hold onto the memories we've created together."

The friends smiled, knowing that this day would indeed be a memory they would cherish forever.

Finally, it was Tansy's turn. Her eyes sparkled as she made her wish, her voice filled with emotion. "My wish is for each of us to know how loved and valued we are. May we always feel safe, happy, and grateful for each other, knowing that we are never alone."

Chapter 23: A Visitor from Beyond the Valley

A soft mist lingered over the Valley of Echoes as the morning sun rose, casting gentle light across the trees and fields. The valley felt quiet and peaceful, a sense of stillness wrapping around every leaf and branch. Ember made his way to the leaf pile with a feeling of anticipation, sensing that today might hold something new and unexpected.

As he reached the clearing, he found his friends gathered around, chatting quietly and enjoying the peaceful morning. Bramble, Hazel, Clover, Midge, Nettle, Pip, Willow, and Tansy greeted him warmly, their faces filled with happiness after the beautiful Harvest Gathering they'd shared.

"Good morning, everyone!" Ember greeted, settling into the leaf pile.

"Good morning, Ember!" his friends replied, smiling back at him.

The group began to discuss their plans for the day, each friend suggesting a new game or a place to explore. But before they could decide, a soft rustling sound caught their attention. It was coming from the edge of the clearing, near a patch of tall grass. The friends turned, their eyes widening as they saw a small, unfamiliar figure stepping into the open.

It was a creature none of them had seen before—a young porcupine with quills that gleamed in shades of brown and white, his eyes wide and curious as he looked around the clearing. He seemed hesitant, as if unsure whether he was welcome. His quills bristled slightly, a sign of his nervousness, but his face held a hopeful expression.

Ember felt a surge of kindness for the newcomer. He remembered how Tansy had looked the first day she'd come to the valley, shy and unsure, and he wanted to make the porcupine feel as welcome as possible.

With a warm smile, Ember waved his paw, calling out in a gentle voice. "Hello there! Welcome to the Valley of Echoes. My name is Ember, and these are my friends. Would you like to join us?"

The porcupine's eyes widened with surprise, and he took a few tentative steps closer. "Thank you," he said softly, his voice barely above a whisper. "My name is Quill. I've been traveling for a long time, searching for a place to call home. I didn't expect to find... well, anyone so welcoming."

Hazel's face lit up with excitement, and she gave Quill a friendly wave. "We're glad you found us, Quill! You're welcome to stay as long as you like."

The friends introduced themselves, each one offering Quill a warm welcome. As they spoke, Quill's quills gradually relaxed, his face softening with relief and gratitude. It was clear he hadn't met many friendly faces during his travels, and the kindness of the group was a welcome surprise.

Once Quill had settled in, the friends invited him to share his story. They were curious about where he had come from and what had brought him to the valley.

Quill took a deep breath, his voice gentle and filled with emotion. "I came from the far hills, beyond the mountains. My family and I used to live in a small burrow near the edge of a meadow. But as I grew, I felt a strong pull to explore, to see more of the world and find my own place. My family understood, but it was still hard to leave. I've been wandering ever since, hoping to find somewhere I could belong."

The friends listened with quiet respect, touched by Quill's story. They understood his desire to find a place where he could feel at home and surrounded by friends.

Willow gave him a gentle smile, her voice full of understanding. "The Valley of Echoes is a place where everyone is welcome. We're a family of friends here, and we'd be honored to have you join us."

Quill's eyes shimmered with gratitude. "Thank you. I've felt lonely on my journey, but today... today feels different."

The friends exchanged smiles, each of them filled with warmth for their new friend. They wanted Quill to feel as though he had found a true home among them.

Hazel, ever the playful one, clapped her paws together. "Quill, would you like to play some of our games? We have a lot of fun ones, and it'll be a great way to celebrate you joining us."

Quill's face lit up with surprise and excitement. "I'd love to! I haven't played a game in a long time."

The friends decided to start with "Leaf Balance," a game where each friend balanced a leaf on their nose and tried to keep it steady as they walked. They thought it would be a gentle way for Quill to ease into their group activities.

Each friend picked up a leaf, balancing it carefully on their nose as they walked around the clearing. Quill was a little hesitant at first, but as he watched the others laughing and wobbling, he felt his nervousness fade. With a smile, he placed a small leaf on his nose and joined in.

Ember watched with pride as Quill relaxed and laughed, his quills softening as he became more comfortable. It was clear that the games were helping him feel like part of the group, and Ember felt grateful for the way his friends embraced Quill's differences with kindness and openness.

After a few rounds of Leaf Balance, the friends introduced Quill to "Twig Race," a game where each friend held a twig in their paw, trying to see who could reach the other side of the clearing without dropping it. Quill had a unique advantage with his quills, easily keeping the twig in place, and the friends laughed as he won round after round.

"I think you have a talent for this game, Quill!" Bramble said with a grin. "Your quills make it almost too easy for you."

Quill chuckled, his face lighting up with joy. "It's true. My quills have been helpful at times. I used to feel self-conscious about them, worried that others might be afraid. But here, I feel like they're accepted."

Midge fluttered over, her voice gentle and encouraging. "Everyone is different, and that's what makes us special. Your quills are a part of you, just like my wings or Bramble's quick paws. We wouldn't want you any other way."

Chapter 24: A Special Welcome for Quill

The valley was alive with the sounds of chirping birds and rustling leaves, and Ember felt a joyful sense of purpose as he made his way to the leaf pile. Today, he and his friends were planning a special surprise for Quill, their newest friend. They wanted to welcome him to the valley in a way that showed how much they valued him and celebrated his uniqueness.

As Ember reached the clearing, he saw his friends already gathered, chatting excitedly about their plan for the day. Bramble, Hazel, Clover, Midge, Nettle, Pip, Willow, and Tansy greeted him eagerly, their eyes sparkling with anticipation.

"Good morning, everyone!" Ember greeted, settling into the leaf pile with a warm smile.

"Good morning, Ember!" his friends chorused, their voices filled with cheer.

After the warm welcome they'd given Quill the day before, the friends had thought it would be wonderful to create a special welcome ceremony, a day dedicated to showing Quill that he truly belonged among them. They wanted him to feel cherished, accepted, and celebrated for who he was.

"We all know Quill felt a bit shy when he first arrived," Ember began, his voice thoughtful. "So, let's make today a day of surprises—fun activities that show him how much we appreciate him. We'll create a welcome just for him."

The friends nodded eagerly, each one brimming with ideas. They quickly divided the tasks, wanting every part of the day to be as special as possible.

Hazel and Clover volunteered to decorate the clearing. They planned to gather colorful leaves, flowers, and berries to create a warm and festive atmosphere. They wanted the space to feel magical, welcoming Quill with the colors and beauty of the valley.

Bramble and Nettle took on the task of gathering food. They would collect tasty treats like acorns, chestnuts, and even some special mushrooms that Quill might enjoy, making a feast that celebrated the abundance of the valley.

Midge and Willow decided to create games specifically designed to include Quill's unique abilities. They wanted Quill to feel confident and celebrated, showing him that his quills were not something to hide but something to be proud of.

Ember and Tansy took responsibility for creating a special keepsake that Quill could carry with him—a gift to remind him of his new friends and his place in the valley.

With their tasks decided, the friends set off in different directions, each one eager to make the day unforgettable for Quill.

Hazel and Clover wandered through the forest, their eyes scanning the ground for the most vibrant leaves, flowers, and berries. They found bright red and orange maple leaves, golden birch leaves, and delicate wildflowers in shades of purple and blue, gathering them carefully.

"We can hang these leaves and flowers in a circle around the clearing," Hazel said, her eyes gleaming with excitement. "It'll make the space feel cozy and festive."

Clover held up a handful of berries, her face full of joy. "And these berries will add a lovely touch. We can use them to create patterns in the leaves."

The two friends returned to the clearing and began decorating. They hung the leaves and flowers along the branches surrounding the leaf pile, creating a circle of vibrant color that made the space feel warm and welcoming.

Meanwhile, Bramble and Nettle were busy gathering food. They found acorns and chestnuts nestled among the trees, their smooth shells glistening in the morning light. Nettle also discovered a few patches of wild mushrooms, carefully selecting the ones that were safe to eat.

"These will make a wonderful feast," Bramble said, his voice filled with pride. "Quill will know how much we care about him when he sees all the food we've prepared."

Nettle smiled, arranging the food in a neat pile. "We're showing him that he's truly part of our family now."

With the food gathered, they returned to the clearing, arranging their collection in the center. The feast looked bountiful and inviting, a delicious treat for everyone to enjoy.

At the same time, Midge and Willow were planning games that would make Quill feel special. They came up with a game called "Quill Toss," where each friend would take turns tossing small rings made of vines, trying to loop them onto Quill's quills. The game was designed to celebrate Quill's unique abilities, showing him that his quills were something fun and special.

"This game will be perfect!" Midge said, her wings fluttering with excitement. "Quill will get to be the star of the game, and we'll all get to celebrate his quills."

Willow nodded, her face glowing with enthusiasm. "And it's a reminder that we all have different gifts, each one making us special."

With the games ready, Midge and Willow joined the others in the clearing, eager to share their ideas with Quill.

Meanwhile, Ember and Tansy were working on their keepsake gift. They wanted to create something that Quill could carry with him as a reminder of his new friends and the valley he now called home. They decided to make a small charm using a smooth pebble, a small feather, and a colorful piece of bark.

Ember held up the pebble, his eyes soft with thought. "This pebble represents the valley's strength and stability. It's a symbol of the friendship we're building with Quill."

Tansy carefully tied the feather and bark to the pebble with a strand of vine, adding a small cluster of berries for color. "And the feather reminds him of our kindness and gentle spirit, while the bark shows the beauty and uniqueness of his quills."

The finished charm was simple yet beautiful, a small token that captured the love and acceptance of their friendship. Ember and Tansy returned to the clearing, holding the charm with pride, knowing it would be a meaningful gift for Quill.

As the preparations were completed, the friends gathered in a circle, admiring their hard work. The clearing looked vibrant and welcoming, decorated with leaves, flowers, and berries. The feast was arranged in the center, and the games were ready to bring laughter and joy to the day.

"Everything looks perfect," Ember said, his voice full of warmth. "Now, let's bring Quill over and start the celebration."

The friends found Quill resting near the edge of the clearing, his eyes widening with surprise as he saw them approach.

"Quill!" Hazel called out, her voice bright with excitement. "We have a surprise for you. Come and see!"

Quill's face lit up with curiosity, and he followed the friends back to the clearing. As he stepped inside, his eyes widened with awe at the sight before him—the decorations, the feast, and the warm smiles of his new friends.

"We wanted to create a special day just for you," Ember said, his voice gentle. "A welcome celebration, to show you how much we appreciate you joining us in the valley."

Quill's eyes shimmered with emotion as he looked around. "I... I don't know what to say. No one has ever done something like this for me before."

The friends gathered around him, their faces filled with love and warmth.

Hazel stepped forward, handing him a leaf decorated with berries. "Today is all about you, Quill. We want you to feel at home here."

They began with the game of Quill Toss, and Quill's face lit up with laughter as his friends tried to loop the vine rings onto his quills. The game was a playful reminder of the joy his quills brought to the group, and he felt a sense of pride in his unique qualities.

Next, they shared the feast, each friend offering him acorns, chestnuts, and mushrooms. As they ate, they shared stories and laughter, filling the air with the warmth of friendship and acceptance.

After the feast, Ember and Tansy presented Quill with the charm they had made. Quill held it carefully, his face filled with gratitude.

"This charm is a reminder that you're a part of our family now," Tansy said softly. "It carries the spirit of the valley and the love of all of us."

Quill's voice was full of emotion as he replied, "Thank you. I feel so grateful to have found friends like you. Today has been one of the happiest days of my life."

The friends relaxed, basking in the joy of the day. They knew that their friendship with Quill had become even stronger, a bond built on kindness, acceptance, and love.

Chapter 25: A Journey of Friendship

The morning in the Valley of Echoes dawned softly, with golden sunlight streaming through the trees and filling the valley with a gentle warmth. Ember woke with a feeling of deep contentment and reflection. It had been an unforgettable season with his friends—filled with games, discoveries, kindness, and love. Today, he wanted to gather everyone together to reflect on their journey, celebrating the friendship that had grown so beautifully over time.

As he made his way to the leaf pile, Ember felt a deep sense of gratitude for the valley and for each friend who had filled his life with joy and meaning. Bramble, Hazel, Clover, Midge, Nettle, Pip, Willow, Tansy, and their newest friend, Quill, had all made the valley feel like home.

As Ember reached the clearing, he saw his friends waiting for him, their faces bright with smiles and curiosity.

"Good morning, everyone!" Ember greeted, his voice warm with affection.

"Good morning, Ember!" his friends replied, gathering closer around him.

Ember settled into the leaf pile, his heart full of love and appreciation. "I was thinking," he began, "about all the incredible adventures we've had together. Every moment we've shared has become a part of the valley's story, and I thought today could be a day for us to reflect on our journey and celebrate the friendships that make this valley feel so special."

The friends nodded, their faces filled with warmth. They each felt the same deep gratitude, knowing that their journey together had been one of laughter, kindness, and discovery.

Hazel's eyes sparkled with excitement as she spoke up. "Let's each share our favorite memory! There are so many to choose from, but

I think it would be wonderful to remember all the joy we've had together."

The friends agreed, and they formed a cozy circle around the leaf pile, each one ready to share their favorite memories.

Ember decided to go first, his voice soft with emotion. "One of my favorite memories was the day we discovered the hidden hollow. It was such a magical place, and making it our own felt like finding a secret part of the valley. It was a moment that reminded me of the beauty of exploration and the joy of sharing it with friends."

The friends nodded, their eyes shining as they remembered the hidden hollow, their sanctuary filled with wonder and peace.

Next, Bramble spoke, his voice steady and warm. "I think my favorite memory was the Festival of Friendship. We decorated the clearing, shared our favorite foods, and celebrated the love we have for each other. It was a reminder of how lucky we are to have each other and this beautiful valley."

The group murmured in agreement, each of them touched by the memory of the festival and the gratitude that had filled their hearts that day.

Hazel was next, her voice full of laughter. "One of my favorite memories was the Harvest Gathering. We played games, caught falling leaves, and ended the day with a circle of wishes. It was a celebration of the season and of everything we love about this place and each other."

The friends smiled, remembering the joy and warmth of that day, knowing it would be a tradition they would cherish for years to come.

Clover spoke up next, her voice soft and thoughtful. "My favorite memory was when we made the Memory Book. Writing down our stories and capturing our adventures reminded me of the importance of friendship and the love we share. It's something we can look back on forever, a reminder of the journey we've taken together."

The friends nodded, each of them feeling the same sense of pride and connection. The Memory Book was a treasure, a symbol of their friendship and the bond that held them together.

Midge, ever full of wonder, shared her memory with a bright smile. "I loved when we found the SkySeekers' marks! It felt like we were connecting with the valley's past, walking in the footsteps of the creatures who loved this place before us. It reminded me that our friendship is part of something much bigger—a legacy of love, kindness, and discovery."

The friends exchanged thoughtful glances, each one feeling a deep connection to the valley and its history, grateful to be part of its story.

Willow spoke next, her voice gentle. "My favorite memory was the day we welcomed Tansy. Seeing her find a home with us reminded me of the power of kindness and the joy of welcoming new friends. Our friendship grows brighter with each new friend we meet."

The friends turned to Tansy, who smiled with gratitude, feeling the warmth of Willow's words. She knew that finding them had changed her life, filling her heart with love and belonging.

Tansy shared her own favorite memory, her voice filled with emotion. "I loved the day we created the Memory Book together, capturing the laughter, the games, and the kindness we've shared. That day reminded me that friendship is a gift that lasts forever, a treasure we carry with us wherever we go."

The friends nodded, each of them feeling the same deep appreciation for the memories they had made.

Finally, Quill spoke, his eyes shining with gratitude. "My favorite memory was the special welcome you gave me. I had traveled so far, feeling unsure and alone, but when I met all of you, I felt like I'd found my family. I've never felt so accepted, so loved, and that day will always hold a special place in my heart."

The friends gathered around Quill, each of them touched by his words. They knew that their friendship had become even stronger with each new member, a circle that grew warmer and more welcoming with every friend they met.

Ember turned to his friends, his voice filled with warmth. "Today has been a reminder of everything we've shared, the laughter, the kindness, and the love that fills this valley. We've become more than friends; we've become a family, bound by the memories we've made and the joy we bring each other."

The friends held hands and paws, their hearts filled with peace and gratitude. They knew that the valley had brought them together, but it was their love, kindness, and acceptance that had woven them into a family.

They decided to end the day with a final entry in the Memory Book, each friend contributing a word that captured the spirit of their journey. Ember picked up a small stick and dipped it into a berry ink Clover had prepared, carefully writing each word on the last page.

Together, Love, Laughter, Friendship, Kindness, Adventure, Family, Gratitude, Memories, Forever.

The friends smiled as they looked at the words, knowing that they captured the essence of everything they had shared. The Memory Book was complete, a collection of stories and moments that would forever remind them of the beauty of friendship.

When it was time to say goodnight, the friends hugged each other tightly, each one carrying the warmth of their journey together. They knew that their friendship was a gift that would last a lifetime, a light that would continue to fill the Valley of Echoes with love and laughter.

Don't miss out!

Visit the website below and you can sign up to receive emails whenever Nora Black publishes a new book. There's no charge and no obligation.

https://books2read.com/r/B-A-KJCVC-QYJIF

BOOKS 2 READ

Connecting independent readers to independent writers.

Did you love *Leo and the Leaf Pile*? Then you should read *Amara's Autumn Adventure*[1] by Bella Moore!

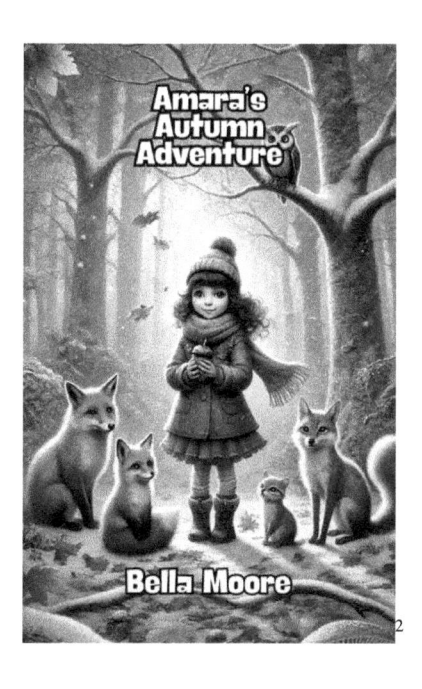

In *Amara's Autumn Adventure*, young Amara embarks on a journey through a magical forest that shifts with each passing season.

Guided by her wise animal friends—Juna the joyful squirrel, Mira the gentle fox, Sable the wise owl, and Finn the shy fox—Amara learns timeless lessons about kindness, resilience, and the beauty of change. Each chapter explores a new experience, from the joy of falling leaves to the quiet wisdom of winter's first snowfall.

This enchanting tale encourages mindfulness, respect for nature, and the warmth of friendship, showing young readers the power of community and inner strength.

---

1. https://books2read.com/u/4AlLPe

2. https://books2read.com/u/4AlLPe

About the Publisher

Lightwave Publishers is dedicated to creating a world of wonder, learning, and imagination for young readers. Specializing in educative and captivating children's books, our mission is to inspire curiosity, foster creativity, and instill positive values. From heartwarming tales of friendship to adventures that teach diversity, inclusion, and resilience, our stories are crafted to entertain while nurturing critical thinking and emotional growth. Each book is thoughtfully designed to engage children aged 5 to 12, featuring vibrant illustrations and relatable characters. At Lightwave Publishers, we believe in the transformative power of stories to enlighten young minds and empower them to dream big.